Fallout Stories

MICHAEL ANDRE-DRIUSSI

ISBN: 1947614061
ISBN-13: 978-1-947614-06-2
****

"Atomic Missions" was first published online at *Kaleidotrope*, January 2015.

"Cyborg Vedohtsee and the Outlaw Slick Polla" was first published at *Scifia #1*, July 2012.

"*Fallout 3* versus *The Omega Man*" was first published at *New York Review of Science Fiction #295*, March 2013.

"Fallout 1979" was first published at *Plasma Frequency Magazine #1*, July 2012.

"The Walking, Weeping Prototypes" was first published online at *Black Denim Lit*, April 2015.

CONTENTS

CUBAN MISSILE STRIKE

Frank Simpson was waiting in a tense line at the bank in Orlando when the lights cut out, but it was four in the afternoon so there was plenty of ambient sunlight through the windows. Then came a roar from the south that removed all doubt.

Screams tore the grim calm.

In a panic, Frank dashed out to the street, where he found the October sky clear of fighter jets for the first time in a week. Spotting his car, a bright red Jaguar XKE, he felt a wash of relief. He just wanted to get home to Mount Dora before traffic got bad. But when he noticed the telephone pole lying across the car, he cried out in despair.

Frank shook himself and reasoned that the car might still work, he might start it and get it out from under its trap. When he reached the door he saw his reflection in the window, a Cary Grant playboy with clear frame glasses. He got into the car and turned the key. Panic returned as, no matter how he tried, the car would not start.

He got out of the car. People were starting to stir, like ants from a ruined nest. The national nightmare had come true in broad daylight, and he faced the disaster he had been blocking from his mind: the mushroom cloud towering to the south showed vibrant red, shimmering orange, and canary yellow. He thought of God; he thought of Dodie, his girlfriend. He wondered if she saw it; he wondered if he would live to see her again. The colors were beautiful, nearly hypnotic, but he had no car and almost thirty miles to go.

Frank started walking, then spun around and returned to the car. From the trunk he took a few road flares and a pair of pliers that he thrust into the pockets of his sports coat. He took up the tire iron before walking away, heading north.

Cars started up; others went past very fast. Some cars collided at the powerless traffic lights, but after a time it was all a traffic jam, like Thanksgiving combined with the end of Spring Break: everybody trying to get home.

Frank kept walking, as did many others. At some point, maybe an hour in, he suddenly wondered about the others in the bank he had left. He had not thought to help them, he had simply bugged out, just like so many of his fellow soldiers had done in Korea. He shrugged it off: he certainly was not going back now.

A city of near ninety thousand people, stirred up like an ant nest. Those who were near McCoy Air Force Base were dead. He was just another ant, walking along to the northwest.

Frank felt the urge for a drink since he had not imbibed since before noon, but the situation was too demanding for that. Maybe all this hiking would cure him, break the year of heavy drinking as completely as that pole had broken the sports car.

Frank had assumed that an atomic war would be the end of the world: that everyone would die like in those horrible images from Hiroshima and Nagasaki. Maybe that would still happen if there were more missiles, but he had been ten or twelve miles from a nuclear explosion, and he had survived.

Sunset came when he reached the town of Lockhart, where a roadside restaurant was cooking up all their meat since the power was out. Frank bought a warm steak, ate it with his hands, and drank some water. It was like a picnic, or an evening at the county fair. He got a couple of aspirin to help his splitting headache, but he knew they would have no effect on the tremors of his hands.

The twilight was deepening when he started out again. The streetlights were dark, but the car headlights were on, and building windows showed light from candles and storm lamps.

Frank was a little surprised that there was no looting going on, as always happened in times of hurricane. It was as if the usual looters, the poorest Negroes and the white trash, knew that this moment was different, somehow sacred.

"Silent night, holy night," he said. "All is calm."

He knew that looters hit liquor stores first, and thinking that, his booze thirst came roaring back. There was a closed liquor store ahead, and he hurried over to knock on the door, hoping to buy a bottle, but there was no answer. He trudged on into the Moonless night, following Highway 441.

Two hours later he was at Apopka, the old Kluxer town. The place was organized, with roadblocks manned by police and civilians with rifles, protecting the town streets from the horde of refugees. There was not much trouble, since most of the travelers were just trying to get home.

It was midnight when he passed through the normally sleepy village of Zellwood. The guardians looked on him with sympathy mixed with curiosity. He asked for water and aspirin, then told them of his travel and answered their questions in exchange for their kindness.

About an hour later he came to the edge of Mount Dora as he skirted first Pistolville, a disreputable community of Minorcans and white trash, and then East Town, the Negro district. It got Frank to musing on the painful memories of his failed mayoral campaign of the year before.

Frank was a lawyer, heir to a family so prominent in Mount Dora that streets and buildings bore their name. But Frank was a new type of Democrat, an anti-segregationist. So even though he had the Negro vote, he still lost to Mayor Logan in a five to one landslide. That defeat in 1961 marked the beginning of his heavy drinking.

But now, on what might be the last night of mankind, all that pain and humiliation he had suffered seemed like foolish vanity.

Finally he was beyond city limits, back into the countryside of Central Florida. Despite his exhaustion, he jogged along River Road. As he approached Simpson Court he saw how a storm lamp lit up a new sign painted on a big piece of plywood: "Fort Simpson. Looters Will Be Shot." The broadside of a car, flanked by two others, blocked the entrance to his cul-de-sac. The sign and the roadblock looked like the work of his neighbor, the old admiral. Frank laughed and called out a hallo.

Headlights from one of the flanking cars blinded him. He heard a car door open, then the sound of a woman running toward him.

"Oh God, Frank," said his girlfriend Dodie, weeping in relief. "We were so scared for you. Thank God, thank God, you made it home!"

•

The morning of November 4 found Frank Simpson sitting on the bandstand at what was already being called "Barter Park," where he watched over the trading of goods and services. The world had changed in those seven days: the people of Mount Dora knew through the radio that Florida had been hardest hit in America, with air force bases near Miami, Orlando, and Tampa struck by nuclear missiles from Cuba. But Washington D.C. had also been hit, an attack that killed President Kennedy. In an automated retaliation, Cuba and the USSR had been destroyed.

Since the world had not ended with the atomic war, Frank adjusted his thinking so that it was the end of America and the dawning of a new dark age that would last for hundreds of years. As such, his goal would be to preserve as much of American culture as was practical in a quasi-medieval setting.

Mount Dora itself was doing fairly well, given the circumstances. City Hall stood empty to the east of the park, the police chief was dead, and the mayor was missing; yet security and governance had been taken up by each neighborhood, making a patchwork of cooperating communities. There had been a fire over at the Sylvan Shores area to the west, but it had burned itself out: a lucky thing, since the loss of electricity from Orlando had halted water flow, among many other effects.

The segregated water fountains at Barter Park were rendered equally non-functional, and when Frank saw a white man drink from a Negro's offered bottle, it struck him as a silver lining to the crisis.

Frank's reverie was broken when a voice beside him said, "Good morning Mr. Mayor."

"No," said Frank, turning to see the somber man, "I'm not the mayor."

"Well, I voted for you."

"You did? Why, thank you. I thought I knew the names of all my supporters — I'm sorry it was so lopsided."

"It happens. It was worth a try. Well, anyway, you're pretty much the mayor now."

"So what can I help you with?"

"I live a few blocks east of here. We've organized the neighborhood and everything, you know, got our new water system worked out, such as it is. And everybody is accounted for, except for one house which belongs to an older couple."

5

"Maybe a suicide, you think?" asked Frank.

"Right, or they're out of town, still trying to get home. Anyway, we'd like to go inside and find out, but we want it to be all, you know, lawful, and so I ask you to come along."

"All right."

They left the park and walked east along Old Highway 441, an avenue lined with trees of palm and leaf. The business district was to the south, where mounted hurricane shutters tried to mask the signs of looting at liquor store, pharmacy, and market. The shops were all empty now, with trading going on over at Barter Park or by private appointment.

They turned left on the residential street, going around the blockade of cars. They passed a few houses on the right, each a single story wood frame construction, with no fences between them.

Their destination was a similar two-story house on the left. Its paned-glass front door was locked. The adjacent windows were locked, as was the side door. Searching for a ladder, they went into the garage, where they found a 1955 Ford Fairlane, a strong indication that the couple was not out of town.

Frank and the man located a ladder and brought it out to lean against the house. On the third try Frank found an unlatched upstairs window. When he opened it, Frank caught the immediate whiff of death.

The couple lay on the bed, holding hands. It looked like a case of poison or drug overdose. Frank went down through the house to let in the man along with the other neighbors who had gathered.

"Why'd they do it?"

"Thought it was the end of the world, I guess," said Frank. "Sure were a lot of suicides on The Day."

The neighbors murmured sad agreement, then one said, "Well, now what?"

Frank organized it. The stuff in the house was property

of the neighborhood, to be administered by the local leader. He recommended that the hurricane shutters be put up to help maintain the house for possible relatives of the deceased, or for rental to later arrivals of displaced persons.

"The bodies should be buried in the yard immediately," he told them. "Those who do the digging should be paid with items from the house, starting with perishable foods."

Two men started digging a double grave while Frank and the leader did a quick inventory of the house. Frank went out and took a turn at digging. They carried the bodies down, each wrapped in bedding, and put them in the hole.

"Dear God, Lord of Heaven, please forgive these two," said Frank. "They were good people, fine people, but they were caught unawares, Lord. They were scared and they were weak. Please show them mercy, Lord. Amen."

The leader offered Frank his pick of bottles in the house liquor cabinet, but Frank refused that temptation, accepting some canned food and cigarettes instead.

•

The weeks went by. Over the radio, President Johnson activated all reserves in Florida, instructing officers to assume command of towns where civilian leadership was missing, and Frank Simpson officially became mayor. He organized the other local reservists into Simpson's Troop, a company of thirty men. They patrolled the streets from Sylvan Shores to the west, Frank's "Fort Simpson" to the northeast, East Town, and Pistolville to the southeast, working closely with the many neighborhood militias.

There were births and deaths. There were weddings, as when Frank married his girlfriend Dodie.

Again Frank adjusted his sense of the long-term effects of the Cuban Missile Strike, now downgrading the disaster to one lasting mere decades. Perhaps just ten years, like the

Great Depression, making a bookend to the boom years of the '40s and '50s.

On December 11, nearly two months after the attack, Frank was sitting on the bandstand at Barter Park. The place was half full: the traders were mainly locals but there were Negroes from East Town offering fresh-killed squirrels and armadillos, and some white trash from Pistolville offering knife sharpening. The corpse of the highwayman executed a few days earlier still dangled in place as a warning to outsiders.

Deputy Gus hurried over to Frank, glancing back to a group of people coming from the west.

"You'll never believe it," said Gus, "it's the mayor — Mayor Logan!"

"You're kidding!" said Frank, stunned. "Where the hell has he been?"

"Turns out they had a private fallout shelter over in Sylvan Shores, big enough for two dozen families."

"Isn't that something," said Frank, his initial surprise giving way to growing resentment and bitterness.

Two men accompanied the mayor: one a famous local big-game hunter, the other a bank president. All three were armed with identical lever-action rifles and wore matching pistols on their hips. They appeared clean, too clean for the new normal, which made them look like kids playing cowboy. The crowd behind this trio was composed of curious onlookers acquired in the miles of walking.

Where had these leaders been when things went bad? Frank decided to open strong.

"Good to see you, Mayor Logan. Haven't seen you in months."

"Hello, Frank," said the older man. His pug nose and his jowls gave him a porcine appearance.

"How's the wife and kids?"

Logan's face paled, etched by lines of grief.

"My children are fine," he said, "but my wife . . ."

"Mrs. Logan died in the catacombs," said the bank

president. "In the shelter."

"I'm sorry to hear that," said Frank, taken aback. Suddenly his line of attack seemed petty and mean-spirited. "My condolences."

"Thank you," said Logan, regaining his composure. "Now that we have emerged, we would like to help. We have supplies and expertise. You have done a good job, from what I have heard and what I can see, but we would like to build on it, bring things back to normal."

"'Normal'?" said Frank, incredulous. "There is no going back — this is 'normal' now."

"This is just another temporary crisis, like Hurricane Donna," said Logan. "The time has come to take down the shutters, clean up the mess, and prosecute the criminals, the looters."

"We have been through a lot," said Frank, his anger rising. "There was The Day itself — I was in Orlando, lost my car and had to walk home. The power went out back then, and we've all had to learn new ways around that. There were waves of refugees, then drug addicts, then highwaymen — and where were you, our leaders? Down in a hole, safe and snug!"

"Would it be better if I were up here to die with you in the fallout?"

"'Fallout'?" said Frank. "What fallout? Listen, I was in the army — I read up on the bomb, and I know there is no fallout from an airburst. So the idea is cockamamie!"

"Tampa was hit, right?" said the hunter.

"Sure. Airburst, just like the others."

"But what if Tampa had been hit with a ground burst, either on purpose, or by shoddy work?"

"I'll tell you," said the bank president. "This whole region would be covered with deadly radiation for months. Your easy assessment rests upon a faith in Soviet technical precision that seems dangerously naive."

"Well," said Frank, "we could have used your help."

"We are here now," said Logan. "Frank, I am asking

you to return civilian government, elected government, to Mount Dora."

•

Florida was a mess. On top of everything else, racial tensions had exploded, in large part because President Johnson was seen as a segregationist "good ol' boy," the opposite of "nigger-loving" Kennedy. In northern Florida the Ku Klux Klan retreated from Saint Augustine after losing a few gunfire skirmishes, but Winter Park, near Orlando, was now a klan town, its Negro population having fled.

The re-instated Mayor Logan brought a slew of new changes to Mount Dora. He re-established the money economy and outlawed barter in the park. He disbanded Simpson's Troop, replacing it with police officers brought in from outside. He built up the business district into a fortified compound, wherein most of the new cops lived. The cops patrolled Sylvan Shores and Mount Dora but not East Town nor Pistolville, two places which began suffering increased crime from outsiders.

Mayor Logan was furious that his mansion had been looted in his absence. He spoke darkly of black market-eers, and alternated a carrot and stick approach in dealing with them: one week he bought looted medical supplies at wholesale cost in exchange for indemnity; another week he simply confiscated looted alcohol. The supplies and the booze went to the business compound.

Logan kept Frank supplied with alcohol. Frank fell off the wagon for a bad week but then crawled up again with a lot of help from Dodie and deep soul searching. He came to realize that Logan was neutralizing him with the booze.

Logan's "Back to Normal" campaign was wildly embraced by a large segment of Mount Dora's population, but to Frank it seemed like a frantically happy face on an increasingly hollow promise. It amounted to a spoils system of ever diminishing returns, too much like the crony-ism of the Great Depression.

But worse, it seemed to be getting darker, more fascist. Frank began sending out feelers to prepare three groups for something worse. He talked to members of his old Troop, he spoke with the Negroes of East Town, and then one afternoon Frank rode his bicycle over to Pistolville to visit Ghita Pacetti.

Pistolville had always been a trashy place, like a third-world town, so its change after The Day had not been as pronounced as the transformation of Mount Dora. In a strange way this made Pistolville feel refreshingly "pre-war" to Frank.

The Pacetti house was now a gangster den, with gun-men guarding the door. Frank left his bike with them and went inside. He and Ghita had been lovers a couple years back, and she had recently inherited leadership of the dis-trict after the mysterious murder of her brother. Frank met the jewelry-bespangled mistress of the house upstairs, in a room with a stack of TV sets along one wall.

"Hello, Ghita. You seem to be keeping the peace around here."

"Yes, thanks," she said, giving him a familiar smile that tugged at his heart. "I haven't seen you in a long time, though. Almost like you're avoiding me."

"Well, I'm married."

"That's right. Congratulations to you and 'Dodie,' isn't it? Sorry to hear you were pushed out by Logan, that bas-tard."

"Right," said Frank, "that's what I came to talk with you about. Logan's up to something, something ugly — I think he's going to attack East Town."

"Is it that bad?"

He nodded.

"Look," he said, "I've been talking to my men, the for-mer members of Simpson's Troop, getting them ready for action. Some of them are in East Town, and I've been talking to Elias over there. He wants to call on some Negroes in Saint Augustine to help."

"Sounds good. Let the darkies do it."

"No Ghita, we don't want outsiders to come in. It would be like the Civil War again. We've got to deal with it ourselves."

"Why?"

"Because after East Town, he will move on Pistolville. We have to stand up with the Negroes against these kluxers."

"Let them kill each other off."

"Come on, Ghita, it doesn't work like that," he said. He ran his hand through his hair in frustration. "There's going to be a winner, and there's going to be a loser. If Elias calls in support, things will be that much worse, and then the army will come in. You think the army will like what you have going on around here?"

"What are you saying?"

"Look at you! Look at all your jewelry. I don't think you had that before The Day. Look at all these televisions — I don't recall you having a TV store before The Day."

"All right —"

"If the army comes in here, they're going to have a very dim view on looters — maybe not as bad as Logan, but bad enough."

"I said all right!"

They stood there glaring at each other. Ghita broke and looked away.

"You want a drink?" she asked. "For old times?"

"Only one. Only to seal the deal."

•

Pain woke Frank into a darkness so total he feared he was blind.

He was lying on concrete. His body hurt all over, evidence of a bad beating. The air was close and still, making him feel he was in a cave. One eye was swollen shut, and his ribs hurt, raising the possibility that one was broken.

He sat up and tried to remember who had attacked him. It was four men, those damn kluxer policemen. They had driven up after he left Ghia's place, and said that Mayor Logan wanted to see him right away. So he got in and they drove across town over to Sylvan Shores . . .

Right, he was in the 'catacombs,' the fallout shelter used by Logan and the other elites. The kluxers were strangers to the place, but they knew where it was. Saying it was guaranteed for privacy, they had led him through the hand-dug exit tunnel, and then they ambushed him.

Frank had to explore, find out the details of where he was. Doing a quick inventory, he was surprised to find his glasses in the pocket of his work shirt. One of the cops must have done it, courteously treating him like a passed-out drunkard.

He reached out and touched a plaster wall. He crawled along the wall to the left, discovering a doorway onto cold tile flooring. It seemed like a shower, a hunch confirmed when he found a drain.

Leaving the shower, his fingers felt the wood of a heavy door on the right. He found the doorknob and used it to haul himself up. The door was sealed, impervious to his weakened body slams. A heavy door seemed unusual for an interior doorway, but maybe it was a jail door. Would the fallout shelter have a jail? Maybe. It seemed to have one now, in that he was locked in. But would a jail have a shower? Maybe it was a gym.

He lowered himself to the floor. The new wall felt like it was made of cinder blocks. He crawled alongside it for a few body lengths, passing where he supposed he had woken up, until he found a corner with a plaster wall continuing to the left. He followed this a short distance to where the wall bent out in a dogleg and his fingers touched wood. It was another heavy door. He struggled up and tried the knob. The door opened inward toward him, a welcome discovery, and in pulling it he found a wall at his back, making this a short narrow corridor at an angle to the first hallway.

Excited, he dropped down to all fours and reached a-head, discovering a step leading up, then another. They were stairs, a way out! He crawled up the stairs until his head bumped on a heavy metal ceiling. He pushed and strained against it, but to no effect. What kind of room was this? It had stairs, so the ceiling must be a door. Meaning the room was like a basement, with a trapdoor at one end and a shower at the other end . . .

It was the shelter entrance, the original way in! The shower was for decontamination. Freedom was right behind this metal door, if only he could raise it.

Frank backed down the stairs and continued following the wall, surprised when it opened onto a chamber on the right. What was this? A room behind the first plaster wall, stretching toward the shower. The place smelled of gasoline, machinery, and oil. Crawling in, he encountered a big machine, an engine of some kind, which he guessed must be a generator.

Okay, he thought, pulse quickened with excitement. *Say this is the electrical generator for the catacombs. What do they do when the power goes out? Old Smitty comes over here, in the dark, and he reaches for the handy flashlight . . .*

Frank stood up, felt around beyond the doorjamb's edge, and then grunted with satisfaction when his hand found a flashlight.

When he turned it on he affirmed that he had not been blinded, and the light revealed his guess about the room was correct. Beyond the generator itself, the beam picked out on the floor a tool belt, a pile of cinderblocks, and a pry bar. Snatching up the bar, he hurried back to the stairs and tried to leverage open the metal trap door. He strained, he gave it his all, but the door would not budge. Discouraged, he left the bar wedged there and went down the stairs again.

Limping along the hallway, Frank saw the place was like he had imagined, except for one incongruous decoration: a big American flag taped onto the cinderblock wall.

Suddenly he heard voices approaching from behind the locked door, and he wished he had kept the pry bar.

There was the scraping sound of a door bar being lifted, then the door swung out and two kluxers came into the hallway, flashlight beams swinging around the empty corridor.

"Where's he?" said the first.

"Can't get far," said the second, his voice echoing in the decontamination shower. "We'll find the nigger-lover."

Ready for an ambush, they looked in the generator room, but he was not crouched behind the big engine.

"Holy shit, he just vanished."

"Wait a second," called the other from the stairwell. "Lookee here! There's a pry bar wedged up there."

"No way, that door's too heavy."

"Come on, give it a try. How else did he get out?"

"Well look, that pry bar wouldn't still be there if he went out."

The klansmen came down the hallway again. Seeing the flag hanging on the wall, the one made an abrupt gesture to the other and pointed at the flag. His comrade nodded and together they rushed over to sweep aside the cloth and shine their lights into the large hole it was covering.

"Damn," said one when the little crypt proved to be empty. "I was sure that was it."

He stiffened with a new thought, and then rushed through the open door into the shelter's communal area, only to stand there, the beam of his flashlight flitting around the wide empty space.

"We better report to the Night Hawk."

"He ain't going to like it."

"Gets worse the longer we wait."

"That nigger-lover's got to be in here, somewhere. We should search it."

"Or maybe he got out, we don't know."

"We need more men to search this place."

"More men? We don't have time for that!"

"I don't want to miss East Town either, but we've got to report. Let them figure it out. Four or five guys could make a quick sweep of the place."

The big room had four corridors opening onto it: two on the left, and two on the right. The cops made a beeline for the first one to their right, rounding the corner of the women's bathroom. As they passed its open doorway their light beams peeked in, illuminating stalls for toilet and showers. Standing behind the door, Frank held his breath, and the klansmen continued down the corridor, inadvertently showing him the way out of the maze.

Frank felt his skin crawl with the memory of his brief stay in the crypt, the place formerly occupied by Mrs. Logan's corpse. Silently he said a brief prayer for her.

•

The night was dry and windy, typical for the season. Frank had to get to East Town, located on the other side of Lake Gertrude. The way south around the water on Old 441 would be a mile shorter but it went through a populated area, so he set out on the northern route.

As he alternated between hiking and jogging, Frank tried to guess the form of the coming attack. Since Mayor Logan was obsessed with looters, Frank considered a "Kristallnacht" sort of action, with the KKK forcefully "repossessing" valuable property, but that seemed silly because the Negroes had little wealth and besides that, they were armed.

That same Negro firepower also seemed to rule out frontal assault, along with the klan's technique of planting bombs at unguarded locations.

The road around the lake turned into River Road and Frank was tempted to go home first. Sure, that meant hiking past the town, but then he could start rallying his troop and pick up another bicycle. He refused it, sensing time was too short for that, and turned south on Highland Street.

Suddenly there was a man in a white robe who said, "Ayak?"

"Oh, hey," said Frank. "I've got a message, urgent message for the Night Hawk. Where is he at?"

"How come you didn't answer right?"

"Sorry, I'm in a hurry to get this message to the Night Hawk."

"What is it?"

"I can't tell you! Where is he?"

"I dunno, down around Lincoln."

"Thanks! We're going to show those niggers!"

Frank jogged toward town as best as he could, fighting the pain. Feeling the eyes of the kluxer following him in the darkness, he knew that a neighborhood watchman would put a light on him in a couple blocks. Since he did not want to be seen having a conversation with a Negro, he cut east onto Pine, one of the two throughways giving a straight shot to Highway 441. Gasping, he walked a block, then turned south onto Orange and approached the neighborhood barricade, turning his flashlight on.

"Who dere?" challenged the sentry.

"It's Frank Simpson," he said, shining the light up at his own face. "I'm looking for Rufus — he on duty tonight?"

"Sure is, he down at da other end. Whas goin' on, mister? You look all beat up."

"Stay alert," said Frank. "Trouble coming."

A block later Frank had a similar opening talk with Rufus and then got down to the battle plan.

"I'm going over to tell Elias. I want you to round up Tyrone and the Sarge, meet me over there, all right?"

"Yes, sir," said Rufus, snapping a salute before running off.

Frank limped toward Lincoln Avenue, the other throughway to Highway 441. At Elias's block the militia sentry recognized him and took him directly to Elias's house where the family was asleep. While Elias was waking up, Frank asked the sentry for two pairs of runners, one to take a message to Fort Simpson, the other to take a message to Pistolville. He wrote out the two notes by candlelight at the kitchen table, where it felt very good to be sitting down.

Elias was shocked by Frank's battered appearance.

"Mister Simpson, who did this to you?"

"Those kluxer policemen, and they're going to attack East Town soon, before dawn, I think."

They sent out additional runners to alert each of the two dozen neighborhoods of East Town, but no sooner was that started when Frank heard commotion to the west and saw house fires lighting up the darkness a block away. The assault had started, and Highland Street was burning.

The reaction was confusion, since the neighborhood defenders were torn between fighting the klansmen and dousing the fires. There was not any water pressure since the electrical grid went down, so fighting the fire was especially difficult.

"You should order the men to pull back a block," said Frank to Elias. "Join forces with us on Orange."

"I'll do that, and better," said Elias. He gave out the word for all women and children of East Town to evacuate for the east.

When the Highland Street fighters came around, Frank asked them about the action.

"They's in groups of five," said one. "Three with rifles, an' one cracker throwing fire bottles, and the last one lighting the bottles for him."

"The leader don't say nothing, he just blows a whistle."

"They all in sheets, and a big ol' cross burning at the middle of Lincoln Street."

Black women and children were streaming east through

yards and backyards, avoiding the streets. Frank tried to estimate the number of black fighters they had in East Town, based on population, and supposed it must be a couple hundred. But they had no training and they were scattered in different blocks, so they were being rolled over by disciplined kluxers using a scorched earth tactic. When Simpson's Troop arrived, if they arrived in time, he would assign each man as leader of a larger group — providing officers.

"I think you should call the eastern militias forward," he said to Elias.

"If I ask them to leave their own homes defenseless, what happens if the klan comes around behind us?"

"I don't think they are doing that. They are all massed together."

Then the fire came to Orange Street, forcing them to retreat another block to Simpson Street. This time Frank lingered with the rearguard, watching the kluxers. He observed how the leader blew whistle patterns as commands, but then the nearest kluxers seemed to spot Frank, a white among darkies. The Negroes were urging Frank to leave, and his shoulder was yanked back, making him spin around, falling.

He saw a blurry movie sideways, as if the projector had fallen over while showing some home movie of a street at night. He thought on how the kluxer tactics were clever: on foot, they got around the barriers; and their fire attack was very successful against a fortified defensive posture designed to prevent looting.

Frank felt he was bouncing, as if he were in the bed of a truck going over potholes.

"Where from the gasoline?" he asked, referring to the firebombs.

"Hang on, mister, we take you," said someone, but that made no sense at all.

Then Frank remembered the catacombs. The place was built to run on gasoline power for six months, and the elites had only stayed there for two months, so they had all that gasoline on hand.

Frank came alert to find a black man bandaging his shoulder. He tried to rise but gentle hands pushed him down into the chair.

"Easy, captain. You was shot."

"Tyrone!" said Frank, recognizing his three black reservists among the other faces crowded around. "Good, you're here. How long was I out?"

"Couple minutes."

"The others here?"

"Just the three of us."

"Listen," said Frank. "The wind is favoring the arsonists, but when dawn comes the wind should quit. The kluxers are clever, and yet, here's an odd thing — they are coming faster than the fire, which puts the flames at their back. That seems to be a mistake, since it forces them forward. They are not burning Lincoln Avenue, meaning this is the southern edge of their action."

"So what should we do?"

"Right," said Frank, shaking his head to clear it. "Tyrone, you go to Pine. Sarge, you go to Jackson. Rufus, I want you at Grant. Each of you take command of the fighters there, and hold the line, but be ready to fall back if necessary."

The men saluted and left.

Frank stood up from his chair on the front porch, got dizzy, and sat down again. Dawn should be lighting the sky but the smoke was thick, providing a constant rain of ash and soot. Half of East Town seemed to be burning.

"We need the back militias to come forward now!" Frank told Elias.

"Things would've been better if we had some help from Saint Augustine!"

"Right now I'd accept help from the Army."

The enemy kept advancing. Some fell but others took their place.

Frank had to order a fallback from Simpson Street. They were running out of town to retreat into, but at last their fighters were being concentrated into a line.

Yet the kluxers also seemed to be concentrating, as if for a final push. The whistler was becoming more frenzied in his movements.

Their retreat had brought Elias's command group to the stretch of Lincoln Avenue kitty-corner to the block-long Public Works Department and across the street from a big park to the south. Frank looked over the open space with an eye to somehow having a group go there for a flanking maneuver. The defenders were in the last row of houses before the Milner-Rosenwald Academy, another open space that would change the pattern of the fighting.

The night wind was just a breeze now, and faint grey light was coming through the smoke. Frank saw movement in the park, dozens of men crouch-running into position. At first he thought they were white militiamen from south of Lincoln who were voluntarily entering the fray on the side of the Negroes, but then he recognized fighters from Pistolville.

"Get ready to push forward," he told the rearguard. He sent runners to alert the others.

The kluxers advanced along Lincoln Avenue. After they passed the Public Works building, the men in the park fired on their flank, and then Frank urged the rearguard to fire on the kluxers. The klansmen halted, sought cover. Another surprise came in the form of two cars speeding down Lincoln from the east. A few riflemen shot at the cars but most of the kluxers broke and ran. Some escaped into the burning streets, but many were struck down, the whistler among them.

Frank and the rearguard charged forward, joining forces with the men from Pistolville. The kluxer retreat turned into a rout.

As the defenders advanced up the street, Frank check-ed the fallen whistler. First taking the kluxer's revolver away, he rolled the man over. When he pulled off the hood he revealed the familiar porcine face of the mayor.

"You Republican!" said the kluxer. "Race traitor! One day you'll learn I was right, when the niggers stab you in the back. The South will rise again!"

Frank called to a Pistolville man he recognized.

"Emilio, can you go to the fire house and get them to come over here?"

"I'll drive the truck myself if I have to." He grinned. "I've always wanted to do that."

"What are we going to do with him?" asked Elias, nodding toward Mayor Logan.

"Put him in jail, I guess. Along with the others we can pick up."

Elias scoffed, shook his head sadly.

"Well, what else then?" asked Frank. "You want me to hang him like the highwayman?"

"You're the mayor again," said Elias. "And he's done more damage than that robber ever did."

"Don't leave me alone with them, Frank," said Logan. "They'll kill me! You heard him!"

"Shut up. Just shut up."

"Mister Simpson, if you take these hoodies to the jail, the police will just let them go because they're all kluxers, too."

"They were all here, on the streets," said Frank. "Now that they've lost, they sure as hell aren't going to come back to town. They're making their ways back to Apopka and Winter Park."

Elias pondered that a moment, then said, "Well, all right then. I hadn't thought it through like that."

There was the flat zip of a bullet passing close by, followed by the sound of the gunshot. Frank crouched down, searching west along Lincoln Avenue for the source of the shot. He dismissed it as a random shot from the retreating klan, but then a movement on the rooftop of the municipal building caught his eye.

"Sniper!" he cried, throwing himself to the ground.

Logan leaped up in a panic, shouting, "Night Hawk!"

The mayor took two steps before being knocked to the ground, his white sheet running red.

Frank saw the sniper retreating from his perch on the roof, and he felt an almost shameful relief. He thought of pursuing the killer in an attempt to bring the klan officer to justice, but with East Town in flames it seemed that he had more pressing tasks at hand. Like organizing bucket brigades from the white neighborhoods that had sat out the fighting.

"I thought I was done for," said Elias. "And you, too. I never would've thought they'd shoot him. In fact, I don't get it."

"I'm not sure," said Frank. "Probably to keep the klan secrets. And I'll bet they will say he was killed by Negroes."

The wind had stilled and sunlight revealed that the fire was not as bad as it had seemed. Frank, wounded yet victorious in the dawn's early light, felt another shift in his sense of the future. On The Day he thought it was the end of the world; then a week later he figured it was a new dark age; recently he recognized it might only last ten years. Now he grudgingly came to accept Mayor Logan's premise that the Cuban Missile Strike was only a bad hurricane's worth of disaster, as he saw people working together to put out the flames, blacks and whites laboring in unity for the common good that day, and a better world tomorrow.

FALLOUT 1979

Nelly stood facing an empty parking lot, a homemade radiation meter in her hand.

"Call it out," said Dick behind her. He sat behind the wheel of the idling station wagon, a '72 Oldsmobile Vista Cruiser.

It was Day Fourteen, two weeks since President Carter told the nation to shelter in place. By the cloudy morning light Nelly read the foil leaves hanging inside the soup can.

"Minus seven and four," she said, her voice muffled by the bandana. She looked up, pushed her glasses into position, and gazed toward the glass and brick front of the Fareway supermarket so many meters away. "We should park closer — like, right at the door."

"Nope," said Dick.

"Why not?" she asked, looking at him. A big reddish-blond jock, he was twenty-nine, six years older than Nelly, and married with kids.

"Security reasons," he said, and Wayne beside him nodded. Lorraine in the back seat, the youngest at twenty-one, rolled her eyes.

"So instead we take more radiation, walking across half the parking lot." She stretched her shoulders, constrained by a borrowed trench coat that was too small.

"Yep," he said, just like a gym teacher talking to a balky kid.

"That's —"

"Time," said Wayne, as he scratched at his long dark sideburn.

"Minus eight and five," said Nelly.

Wayne looked at the chart and said, "One point six per hour."

"You're kidding," said Dick, as Wayne wrote it down in the notebook beneath the other figures. "Well, damn, we got a local hot spot. We'll give it three more minutes."

Nelly looked around, this being her first visit to Fort Dodge, Iowa. Even though it was now located inside the fallout plume stretching from South Dakota across northern Iowa, the place didn't look all that different from Ogden, a small town eighty kilometers away to the south. In both places the sky was cloudy, and the temperature felt more like fall even though it was summer.

The difference was the total lack of people, the eerie silence of an empty city. On the pavement she saw many little clumps that were dead birds.

"Time."

"Minus eight and six."

"Yeah, not so hot, like point six," said Dick. "So it's probably point six, or average the two readings for one rad."

"Better safe than sorry," said Nelly.

"Okay, so call it 'one.' We're cleared for six hours of work here, minus the driving time, but I doubt we'll be here an hour."

Dick turned off the engine. Nelly put the meter in the back seat as the others got out and stretched.

"That's five times what it was at the spot checks," said Nelly.

"We'll find out later, when more numbers come in," said Wayne.

Dick took up the rifle, put on his John Deere cap, and sat on the hood.

"Hey, bring me some Little Debbies on the first trip out, okay?"

"Sure."

The three scavengers started across the parking lot. Now Nelly saw the dead birds as being subtle signals that this was an area with a lethal cumulative dose in two weeks. Such a dose was more than enough to kill a person, but staying in a house would cut that dose in half. Nelly tried to recall the charts she had studied. Grudgingly she admitted to herself that Dick was right to be security conscious — there could be stranded survivors who would take the car to escape.

"Remember," she said, "powdered milk for the kids. And Tang, we all need the Vitamin C."

"Space Food Sticks," said Lorraine. Her hair was like a shaggy white poodle, a perm growing out. She adjusted her bandana and laughed, saying, "God, we look like bank robbers."

"Get your carts from inside," said Wayne. "They won't be contaminated."

The interior of the supermarket was dark, and Nelly coughed at the heavy odor of rotting fruit and vegetables. They switched on their flashlights.

"First up is a trip to the powder room," said Lorraine.

"Me, too," said Nelly, breathing through her mouth. "For 'security reasons.'"

"Women," muttered Wayne, getting a shopping cart.

"Go ahead and start without us," said Nelly. "Pick up three nine-kilo bags of rice, and some Little Debs."

"Yeah, well, check the phone. It would be good if we could call in from here."

As the women moved toward the back of the store they came across evidence of minor looting.

"Whoever did it must've headed to Wisconsin," said Nelly. Her stomach growled as she caught the smoky scent of fire-roasted meat.

"Yeah," said Lorraine. "I can't imagine stopping at the market, myself, can you? Once I left the house, I'd just drive straight out."

"Hello?" came an old man's voice from the darkness ahead.

The women froze. Nelly found the revolver in her hand but didn't remember drawing it.

"Hello!" she said. "Who's there?"

"It's Howard," said the voice, beyond the open doorway to the backroom. "I'm Howard. Who are you?"

"I'm Nelly, and this is Lorraine, and here comes Wayne. We're from Ogden, down by Boone. Are you a-lone?"

"Well, just me and Dave, but he's dead. The radiation got him."

"How long you been here, Howard? This is Wayne."

"Pleased to meet you. Uh, what day is it?"

"It's Day Fourteen," said Nelly, "August twenty-fourth."

"Oh, then I've been here close on two weeks. Listen, if I help you load up your car, can you take me with you? I mean, you're here to loot the place, right?"

"We're not looters," said Wayne. "We're from Boone County, and Fareway's headquarters is in Boone."

"Oh, I see, I see. So I've been guarding it for you, even though it looks like I've been squatting. Anyway, if I help, can you give me a lift?"

"Yeah, we can," said Wayne. "But that'll be a hundred kilos of food we can't take 'cause of you."

"I'll make it worth your while."

"Of course we'll take you," said Nelly. "Do you have experience in medicine, or police work?"

"Nope. I'm a retired accountant."

"Were you ever in the military?"

"No, I'm four F with flat feet."

"Do you have any family in Boone?" asked Lorraine.

"Nope."

"Any family at all?"

"Just my wife, but she died some years back."

Wayne shook his head and whispered, "It's coming out of your share."

"It's all right," said Nelly to the hidden Howard, "I'll sponsor you, personally."

•

Nelly pushed her loaded cart out the door and shouted, "Hey, we found a survivor!"

"You're kidding!"

Howard came out, pushing a cart, and said, "Hello, I'm Howard."

"Wow," said Dick. "Wow! How're you doing, Howard?"

"Not too bad. Things are looking up."

"You got any high value skills?"

"No," said Wayne, next in line. "Just another loser like us."

Once they reached the station wagon, Howard said, "As a matter of fact, I've got some information that you might want."

"Yeah?"

"Yes. How much weight can this car carry?"

"With four passengers, around 400 kilos," said Dick. "With five people, I dunno . . . how much do you weigh?"

"So each trip you take around 400 kilos? Which is what, 800 pounds?"

"Almost 900."

"There's a dead truck driver back in there, name of Dave," said Howard. "He was alive when I got here, but he had radiation sickness and died after a week.

"Anyway, he was driving on Interstate 24 when he saw the mushroom cloud at Des Moines. In the confusion he drove his truck into a ditch, where he passed out or something, maybe a concussion. When he woke up, the truck wouldn't start, so he got out and walked to the next stop on his list. He ended up here."

"So what?" said Wayne.

"So there's a truckload of food on Interstate 24, west of here, right?" said Nelly. "Maybe the truck can run, too."

Howard nodded. "Dave kept saying it was the battery. Now, with your car here, we could go get a fresh new truck battery at Montgomery Wards just a couple miles up the street."

"I say we do it," said Nelly.

"Well, who's gonna drive it?" said Dick. "You?"

"Damn straight."

"I don't like it," said Wayne. "We've got a guaranteed thing right here, a whole bunch of car-loads. Once we get back to Ogden, the next team takes the car, and we're done for a couple days. Why should we go off on a wild goose chase?"

"How much do you think a twenty-six foot box truck can haul?" asked Howard.

"You tell me," said Wayne.

"Somewhere around 3,000 kilos, I'm guessing. Which means that in one trip today you can deliver many times what you could haul in this one car. But think about it — this truck got its cargo from some sort of food distribution center, right? You find that place later in the week, and then the box truck will really come in handy."

"My God," said Nelly, her mouth watering. "We have to go for it. I say we get the battery and drive along Interstate 24 for an hour or two, using up our exposure time, and if we can't find the truck, we head home with what we got here."

There was a pause.

"Yeah, all right," said Dick. "But we've got mileage limits on one tank of gas, so forty kilometers west, that's it."

"Great," said Nelly, flashing a smile.

•

The trip to Montgomery Wards was quick and easy with Howard giving directions. They picked up two truck batteries of differing sizes, just to make sure.

They found the box truck thirty-two kilometers away, in a shallow depression between the highway and a cornfield. The bad news was that the area had collected so much rain runoff that the truck sat in the middle of a small pond.

Nelly stood with her borrowed rain boots in the water, stunned at how rapidly the foil leaves flexed inside the can. Her mind racing, she called out numbers that made it clear that the water surrounding the truck was another localized hot spot, much more radioactive than the first one.

"We could draw straws," said Dick.

"Absolutely not," said Nelly. "This is my deal. Pace off five meters from the edge, and stay behind that line. Behind the car. That'll cut your exposure in half."

As they moved to comply, she shoved the soup can into her coat pocket and walked further into the water.

"Whoa, wait a minute!" said Lorraine.

"First thing is to see if there's anything inside!" Nelly called over her shoulder, heading to the back of the truck. When she lifted up the door she gave a whoop of joy that was echoed by the others.

"Now check for the keys!" cried Howard.

Nelly hurried around the corner. She stumbled, making everyone gasp, but she recovered without falling into the radioactive soup.

"That's two minutes," said Dick as she reached the door.

Nelly climbed up and felt a trickle of sweat skate down her side. She cried out in triumph at finding the keys in the ignition. She turned the key, but nothing happened. The knob for the headlights was pulled, so she pushed it in. She turned the radio knob until it clicked off.

She tried to keep calm and focused on each task ahead, but every simple thing became more complicated. In growing irritation she searched for the way to open the hood — having succeeded at that, she was propping it up when Wayne called out "Five minutes."

That was too short for what she had gone through, but it was also distressingly long to be exposed to radiation. Her heart raced and she felt a rush of sweat. She looked over to the team to complain but shouted instead at the sight of smoke rising from a farmhouse off to the northwest.

Nelly ran out of the puddle as Dick climbed onto the roof of the station wagon for a better view. The smoke had already grown to a greasy yellow mass, the sign of a house fire.

"Wish we had some binoculars," he said.

"Shouldn't we go help them?" asked Lorraine.

"Hell no," said Wayne.

"I just hope they don't come this way," said Dick. "We've got to hurry."

"Yeah," said Nelly, "so give me the wrench, or whatever."

All they had was a pair of pliers.

Nelly said, "Dick, you keep a watch on that fire, okay?"

"Yeah."

"And Wayne, keep calling my time."

"Sure."

Nelly went back out to the truck and wrestled with the nuts at the battery's post clamps, then fought against the securing bolts. Once it was free, she eagerly started to lift the battery and was surprised at how heavy it was. As she staggered with it across the puddle, Wayne called out "Ten minutes."

Back at the car, Nelly set the dead battery down and reached for the fresh one, but Howard put his hands on it. "Let me help you. I can carry it over."

"No," she said. "You've had more radiation than any

of us. You'll get sick if you get much more."

A number of gunshots rang out from the burning farmhouse. Nelly heaved up the fresh battery and waddled back to the truck. She dropped it into the rack, tightened the tie down finger tight, and started working on attaching the clamps to the posts. Sweat dripped into her eyes, and she couldn't wipe them because her glasses were in the way. The glasses were fogging up and she felt like crying because she was running out of time.

There was a bang and a flash and her arm hurt like hell. She thought she had been shot. The pliers rattled through the engine compartment to splash into the soup.

"You okay?" shouted Lorraine.

"Yeah," said Nelly, figuring it out. "I just touched the pliers to metal and it sparked."

There was no time. She slipped a small plastic bag over her hand and fished the pliers out of the water. Her arm trembled, but she made herself continue the job.

She slammed the hood and climbed into the cab. Wayne called out, "Twenty minutes!"

Nelly flashed them a crossed fingers from the driver's seat.

She turned the key. The engine turned over but it wouldn't start.

"Come on, damn it!" she cried, trying again.

She tried a third time, then pounded on the steering wheel in frustration.

"Hey, can you smell gas?" called Wayne.

Nelly sniffed and, finding the aroma of gasoline, said, "Yeah?"

"Then it's flooded," said Wayne.

"Come on back here," said Howard. "You've got to give it time to dry out."

She went over to the car. Lorraine handed her rags and she wiped off her boots. She sat on the hood, rocking with impatience. They heard motors starting up over at the farm, and to Nelly that sound seemed to mock her efforts.

"How far away is that house?" she asked.

"I don't know," said Dick, "a kilometer?"

Nelly felt sick.

Time dragged on. Finally Dick said, "Okay, Nelly, give it another try."

She walked over, climbed into the cab, and sat there for a moment.

She turned the key. The engine turned over but didn't start.

"Please . . . please," she murmured, her voice cracking.

She tried again. The engine sputtered to life.

Nelly drove the truck out of the puddle, then stopped it and let it idle as she hurried back to the car for decontamination rags.

"All right!" said Dick. "Now let's get the hell out of here!"

"Ten-four good buddy," she said. "Lead the way. Come on, Howard, you're riding with me."

Once they were inside the truck, Nelly said, "Far out! We did it! Now we can talk turkey."

"You don't trust the others?"

"I do," she said, watching the car pull ahead of them, "but I've got to fill you in, and it's easier in private." Nelly had a time grinding the gears, and then they set off with a lurch.

"Sure, I understand that. So are you from Missouri? I noticed the car's license plate."

"That's not my car," she told him. "I'm from Arizona, originally. Went to college in Illinois, wound up in Des Moines. The car belongs to Jane. On Day Four she piled the kids into the car and took off north, drove out of that plume. Now she's part of our shelter group in Ogden, and she let us use her wagon for the job in exchange for a cut.

"I was delivering legal papers when the missiles came on Day Zero. I had a job with this law firm, and even though delivering papers wasn't in my job description, they said I'd be back in Des Moines in time for lunch.

"And Dick! He was coming back from camping with his little family. Saw the mushroom cloud at Sioux City in his rearview mirror — came that close to being in the middle of it.

"But here I am, running like a motor mouth," said Nelly. "Tell me about yourself. Why'd you go to the market?"

"'Cause I ran out of food."

"Makes sense. Did you ever get sick? You know . . ."

"Yeah, I know," said Howard. "I saw it all with Dave. Believe me, I know. The answer is no, I didn't get sick."

"Huh. So, like, you decontaminated, and all that?"

"Sure. I wore trash bags over my shoes, and fixed another one like a poncho."

"How did you know to do that?"

"Just civil defense stuff from the '50s."

"Huh," said Nelly.

"But I've never seen anything like your meter. Can I look at it?"

"Yeah, sure. Here."

It was a soup can with a clear plastic cover that had a number line with zero in the center. Inside, two threads in parallel crossed the middle of the can, each supporting a separate leaf of bent foil. After looking it over, he asked, "What's that in the bottom?"

"Bits of drywall."

"How does it work?"

"I don't know, it just does," said Nelly. "After you set it up, you read the leaves. See the foil hanging from the threads? See the number line? That's in millimeters. So you read off the position of the leaves at the start, you know, to the left and the right of the center, and you time it for a while, then you read the positions again. If there's radiation, it will make the foil leaves open up."

"The leaves look all opened up now," said Howard. "Bigger than the number line."

"Well sure," said Nelly. "It keeps reading the whole

time. The point is what the reading was during the measuring time. We'll have to reset that one."

Howard studied it another moment, then set it down between them.

Trying to sound nonchalant, Nelly said, "So, what was it like with Dave?"

"Well, he had been sick before I got there, but he thought he was better. You know, weak, but better. Then, it must've been a week later, he got it again. Puking, the runs, and the rest."

"Must've been scary."

"I gotta admit, I thought it meant that the store was radioactive." He looked out the window at the poisoned cornfields rolling by. "That I would be next."

"And now we know — he walked all those kilometers, and the first fallout landed straight on him. Poor guy."

"His wife and kids were at Des Moines."

"Ugh," said Nelly. "He'd seen the worst. But with his help, we're still alive."

"We should give him a proper burial."

"You're right, a hero's burial in Ogden. And you, another hero, you're in our shelter group now."

"I'm glad to be there. Or 'here.'"

"It's called 'Griswold's hundred,' because everyone's been put into groups of a hundred, with forty locals and sixty 'visitors.' Our group's in twelve houses at the 700 block of West Cherry. Mr. Griswold's our boss, and Boone is our county seat, thirteen kilometers away."

"Wow, sounds very organized," said Howard.

"Yeah, it's been a rough couple of weeks. The town's population doubled with all the refugees, and then we had to turn the new ones away. That's why Wayne was being that way about taking you in."

"Huh. Okay." Howard absently picked up a small book from the dashboard.

"So you've got to make yourself useful, all right? This truckload and the food distribution place is a great start, but you can't just rest on that."

"Hey," said Howard. "This is his log book — here are the addresses!"

"You keep it. That's all you've got to bargain with."

"Thanks, Nelly."

"I want to get that food, too. I mean, here we are, 'visitors,' busting our butts out in the plume to prove ourselves, our worth, I guess. Well, that's one reason — Lorraine's with us because she likes Wayne. We're getting hazard pay, but money's kind of abstract these days, and we all know that food is worth more than gold right now."

"So what's your reason?"

"Okay — well . . . look," said Nelly. "Each shelter group has a mix of dependents and providers. So, like, we've got Jane and other mothers, and their kids — they're dependents. Plenty of locals are dependents. So there's that fact.

"Now, Lorraine wouldn't mind being a dependent, but I couldn't stand it. I don't want to help out with the kids while 'the men' go out and bring home the bacon. I don't like kids and I certainly don't want to have any — I'm a firm believer in the E.R.A., and I don't like the sort of 'caveman' mentality that's been growing stronger since the nukes."

"And now you're bringing home the big bacon," he said.

"Got that right! 'We got a great big convoy, ain't she a beautiful sight.'"

The irradiated landscape looked brighter to her then, lit by rays of optimism. She had ventured into the dead wasteland and won a treasure.

She turned to him and said, "When we get to Pilot Mound we'll be out of the plume."

Some time later they heard Wayne on the CB radio calling the Pilot Mound check point. After a few calls, the checkpoint responded, and then Wayne explained they were bringing in a new truck and a survivor.

It was around eleven o'clock when they arrived at their shelter group. They went through decontamination by showering and putting on fresh clothing, then they drove their cargo downtown to Clark's Food Mart on West Walnut. It was during the unloading that Nelly vomited.

Dick hurried her over to the fire department, two blocks away. Once a paramedic was assigned to her, Nelly told Dick to go back and make sure they were not being cheated at Clark's.

"It's probably just the flu," said Nelly to the paramedic. "Or maybe nerves."

"Maybe," he said, readying a pen and clipboard.

He asked her questions about her trip. It was all routine until he asked her for the reading on the puddle and she said, "Six."

He raised his eyebrows. "Did you drive into South Dakota?"

"No, of course not."

"Because that's what they say is the average around the craters."

"I know."

He looked back to his clipboard and asked, "How long did you stay?"

"Half hour."

"Then you drove back?"

"Yes."

"Another hour."

"No, more like two."

"Okay," he said, writing a bit. "Well, it looks like you had about four rads. Shouldn't be a problem —"

"Like I said."

"Maybe it is just a bug or nerves. But it is suspicious that you threw up three hours after that last hot spot. That sounds like radiation sickness."

"How hard is that 'six rads per day' rule, anyway?"

"I don't really know," he said. "But if you were a refugee from Missouri, based on your symptoms I'd guess you had absorbed 100 or 200 rads during your drive over. But that's not possible, right?"

"Right," said Nelly, licking her dry lips. "Listen, there was another guy at the store. Howard was with him when he got the second part of radiation sickness, about a week ago. Anyway, my question is, how many rads did he have?"

"Hard to say. He was sick, then better, then sick again, and he died?"

"Yeah, like that."

"Sounds like it was probably more than a thousand," said the paramedic. "But it might have been as low as two-fifty."

Nelly went back to Clark's Food Mart. Since the station wagon had been unloaded, Dick offered her a ride to the shelter group.

"You okay?" he asked, as they started out.

"The medic agrees it's probably just nerves," she said, rolling down the window. "It's been a big day."

"Sure has, but now the team's spooked."

"Don't worry. Send the car out with the next team."

"I think we should wait until the truck is empty, then send it back with a full team in a small car. Or maybe two—"

Suddenly Nelly leaned over and vomited out the window.

"Sorry about that," she said, wiping her mouth with the back of her hand.

"It must've been the puddle," he said, pounding the rim of the steering wheel.

"Maybe. Listen, I don't want to go to the fallout ward, all right? I want to heal up at the shelter group. I can have a little quarantine room, or something, okay?"

"Well, I don't know . . ."

"Promise me."

"All right."

•

The moment Dick left her in her new sickroom, Nelly's arm began to tremble and her stomach knotted up. Fearing another episode, she opened one of the covered buckets and knelt over it, panting and sweating. Nothing came up. She groaned, thinking of the choice she had made which could not be changed, but then she broke into a cold sweat at the new choice before her.

On shaky legs she stood and began pacing. She lost all track of time, so when a gentle knock came at the door she stopped as though she had walked into a wall.

"Nelly?" asked Dick through the door. "Can you handle visitors now?"

"Yes," she said. "Yes, please come in." The door opened and she saw the other three behind Dick. "All of you. Has the second team come back yet?"

"They just left."

"Like we said, the truck and a worker car?"

"Yeah, like that."

"Great." She moved around them and closed the door. "I — Howard, you gotta help me out here. You've got experience, and I — I've got radiation sickness."

"It could be the flu —"

"No," she said. "It's radiation. I just don't understand how I can be sick."

"It was that puddle, wasn't it. I should've gone in there — I'm older, it doesn't matter for me."

"No, it was my deal. I made the choice, but I can't figure out how this happened." She caught herself wringing her hands and stopped. "I mean, well, I got something like 200 rads today."

"Two *hundred?*" said Howard. "How's that possible, when you were talking about ones and sixes? You said the puddle was a twelve."

"I lied."

"God damn it!" said Wayne.

"What?" said Howard. "Then what was it, really?"

"It must've been 400. I just can't figure how."

"But what did the meter say?" asked Howard.

Dick said, "It only goes up to forty, anyway."

"Oh God."

"I figured if it was fifty or eighty," said Nelly, "I'd limit myself to a half hour and get only half as much. More than six, but less than a hundred."

"And we were standing next to that," said Wayne, "so we took a lot, too."

"Yes," said Nelly. She took a shuddering breath. "I had you pace it off, remember? And I told you to keep on the other side of the car. That was about five meters, far enough that you got only half of what I got."

"So wait, I got a hundred?" cried Lorraine.

"Maybe," said Nelly, nodding with sadness.

"This is bullshit," said Wayne. "We need to know the real number."

"Yeah, that's right," said Dick. "We've got to borrow a Geiger counter from Boone, go back and check it out. Then we'll know for ourselves, and for Nelly, too."

"Let's go," said Wayne, and they left.

"I can't believe this," said Lorraine. "I know *you* don't want to have kids, but I'd like to keep my options open."

"I'm sorry," said Nelly. "I'm really, really sorry. I wasn't thinking right. I was only thinking about the risk to me. We said before — when we saw Carter on TV, and we knew we were on our own, we all said that it was death by starvation in weeks or death by cancer in years."

"Yeah, well, there's another one in-between, which is called 'genetic damage.' So you can fry your eggs all you want, but when you fry *my* eggs, without even asking me, that makes me mad!"

Lorraine stormed out, leaving only Howard and Nelly.

"How could a puddle be 400 *per hour?*" she asked.

"It's just like the parking lot," he said. "In the car the guys were saying how the rain probably washed the fallout off the roof and dumped it all onto the lot. It became concentrated. Except instead of being one supermarket roof, it's that whole cornfield, or many fields, feeding into that one puddle."

"But it's more than fifty times the average at Ground Zero, and I don't think we were standing in a crater!" She shook her head suddenly as a new thought occurred, then, looking at Howard with deep concern, she said, "You took 100 today, too — how do you feel?"

"I'm okay."

"Oh God, Howard, I'm so sorry."

Howard sighed. "Maybe it is just the flu."

After Howard left, Nelly threw herself down onto the cot and cried herself to sleep like a little girl.

•

As Nelly suffered through her illness the next day, Dick and Wayne took a technician to the puddle and returned with a solid number — the spot emitted two hundred and twelve rads per hour, meaning Nelly had received around one hundred and the rest of the team had gotten about fifty. Nelly was not in danger of the more advanced sickness that had killed the trucker Dave, but her convalescent period was still set for two weeks.

Nelly kept up on the salvage operations and sent out a pair of motorcycle scouts to investigate the food distribution center that trucker Dave had come from. They returned with news that the place had burned down to the ground, a big disappointment to Nelly.

On the fourth day she felt recovered from her sickness, and the town gave her a victory parade. Mr. Griswold drove the truck and Nelly sat beside him, waving to the thousands of people who lined the streets. Leading the way was Jane's station wagon with the rest of the team, Lorraine and Howard throwing candy to the children.

"Isn't this a bit much?" Nelly asked Mr. Griswold.

"Nonsense," he said. "You're a hero, their first hero. They're afraid you might die, their first martyr. You aren't going to do that, are you?"

"I — I hope not."

"Then we should celebrate! We all need something to celebrate."

Nelly felt uneasy at the accolades that seemed to white-wash the terrible mistakes she had made, but after a few more blocks she realized that she was a symbol to them, a symbol of courage and hope. It wasn't *her*, it was what she represented. This made her feel a little better, but it was seeing Lorraine laugh as she leaned out the window that really gave her relief, and the parade became a wonderful thing.

Then it was back to work.

As the days rolled by, she sent teams to Fareway super-markets in the plume, first to Webster City, near Fort Dodge, and then further afield. The Fareways at Forest City and Clear Lake, at the northern edge of the plume, were already nearly emptied by scavengers from North-wood, Mitchell, and Floyd. On the other hand, Algona's Fareway in the center of the plume was a rich haul, so big that Nelly invited another shelter group in on it.

On the morning of Day Twenty-Eight she approached Dick and said, "My recovery time is over — I want to get back out there."

"No," said Dick. "You're not going into the plume."

"What do you mean?" she asked, bewildered.

"You've been sidelined by injury. You've hit your lim-it."

She looked into his face, hoping he was joking, and said, "But —"

"You see that, right?" asked Dick. "You can't get sick like that again."

"But — but what will I do?"

"What you're doing now."

"This is it?"

"Yeah," he said with a chuckle. "But it seems to get bigger every day. Like this job today you're so eager to ride with."

"I worked hard to set it up, and I don't want any screw-ups at Emmetsburg."

"You're going to have to trust us, and the teams from the other shelter groups."

She felt her face get hot with anger. It was all slipping away from her — despite her dedicated efforts, even despite how she had risked her life at the puddle. She said, "I didn't picture myself like this. It feels like a prison."

"We've all had to make adjustments since Day Zero."

Somewhat chastened, she said, "Sure, but this is like being a . . . " She thought 'housewife,' but instead she said, "An office worker, and I wanted to be out there, doing."

Suddenly it hit her — the office workers she had left behind, the ones she was going to have lunch with later that day, until the mushroom cloud came. She felt guilty and sick, that she had grudgingly taken a chore to deliver papers but had survived when she should have died at the office with the rest.

And now she kept trying to run from her new home, as if they might nuke Ogden at any minute.

"Hey, you okay?" asked Dick.

"Yeah," she said weakly. "Just . . . Day Zero."

"I don't know," said Dick, changing the subject. "It seems to me like you've been promoted. I mean, you've taken over our salvage operations, and now you're even controlling the operations with other groups as well."

"I guess you're right," admitted Nelly. "I hadn't thought of it like that, I just wanted to go out again." She thought of the parade, and how the people thought she had taken those risks for them, not for her own ego. She sighed and said, "Yeah, all right."

"Take it like a man, Nelly. Take it like a man."

She punched him in the arm, which made her feel better.

EURO-NUKE '79

Todd Michaels awoke with a start to find the night lit by a small sunrise over to the north, on the other side of Munich. Nuclear war had finally come, in September of 1979.

As he grabbed up his flashlight, his ears popped painfully and the window glass shattered in a shockwave roar. Todd made a quick round of the boys' dorm, alerting the leaders of grades seven through twelve. They were afraid, but they trusted him and would follow him.

He wished he had a plan worthy of their faith. Through idle talk over three years on the job he knew that nuclear war evacuation drills had been a regular part of dorm life in the 1960s, but such exercises had not been performed in ten years. While Cold War tensions mounted the last few weeks, Todd had looked into those old Alert Plans with longing.

At the moment he needed a few buses for transporting about a hundred American children across West Germany and through France.

Back in his room, he threw on some clothes. He left the building to visit the girls' dorm next door. By his watch he saw it was about 3 A.M.

Josephine Wells, dorm mother, met him at the door.

"Looks like this is it," he said.

"Yes. What should we do?"

Todd was reassured at her cool competence.

"I'm going out to get some buses. You gather up the C-rations and stand by."

She nodded and said, "I'd like to move the girls in with the boys so I can supervise them all under one roof."

"Great idea," he said.

When Todd drove his yellow Fiat through the pre-dawn streets he was encouraged by how light the traffic was, and he envisioned getting a jump on the refugees that were bound to be streaming west, away from the advancing communist forces from Czechoslovakia and Hungary. All he had to do was get the buses and drivers; in a way it was like any Friday when the dorm kids were bused back to their military families for the weekend. He figured that by dawn they would have a convoy leading the wave west.

It did not turn out that way. To the contrary, it took him all day to secure one fully fueled bus, one unmarried driver, and a lot of expired C-rations. It felt like bitter failure, but Todd reminded himself that riding in a bus would be better than walking. He also counted their blessings at being alive, just miles away from an explosion that probably killed a third of the people in Munich.

So they set out on Day Two, with 106 students of the Munich American High School packed in a military bus rated for 50. This olive-drab vehicle entered the river of refugees flowing west toward Stuttgart, 136 miles away. While Todd had heard that Stuttgart had also been nuked, along with Nuremberg to the north, he hoped that they would find more buses at the American High School in Stuttgart.

Cars flooded Highway 8, bumper to bumper, moving across the rolling green plains of Bavaria with the stark Austrian Alps at the horizon to the South. Being Germans, they kept the one lane on the left open. Half of the refugees wore signs of wounds: makeshift bandages, arm slings, and the like. Wrecked cars were pushed off the road, becoming obstacles for the foot traffic to flow a-round.

The bus crawled along, stopping for toilet breaks, and by mid-morning it had passed the leading edge of foot refugees. At noon the bus halted for a lunch of C-rations: the group was so large they ate nine cases of C-rats per meal. The kids learned to cook using canned peanut butter as a makeshift Sterno; the adults learned to collect 106 mini packs of cigarettes. When they stopped for the night the females slept inside the bus while the males slept outside. They were at Günzburg, having covered about seventy-five miles.

Todd Michaels felt his bus strategy had been validated, knowing there was no way they could have walked that distance in two days.

In the morning they started up again. As they completed six miles, Todd and the driver spoke of getting fuel at the base in Ulm or Göppingen ahead. Josephine Wells sat at the midpoint of the bus where she could maintain order.

Soviet planes screamed overhead. Far ahead a lumbering plane dropped a trail of aerial mushrooms, Soviet paratroopers in advance of the Warsaw Pact Armies. Suddenly a fighter plane swooped in from the left, and the front of the bus erupted in shattered glass and flying metal.

•

The driver was dead. Todd Michaels was dead. Worse that that were the three dead kids, little twelve-year-olds who had been sitting at the front of the bus.

Josephine Wells was in charge now. The group took their luggage, the C-rations, the first aid kit and tool kit from the bus. There was no time to bury the dead, no time to mourn.

Josephine wished she had paid more attention to the

discussion and the planning. She had the blood-splattered map now. She knew the men had been talking at breakfast about bases in Ulm and Göppingen.

Now the school refugees were on foot. Sometime soon, in days or hours, Warsaw Pact tanks would push the shot-up bus off the road. The students had to keep moving, to stay ahead of those tanks.

She organized the children as if they were on a field trip, using the buddy system. This made a double line of about fifty. She set up the senior jocks as an advance guard and a rearguard, and she put the seventh graders in the middle, followed by porter teams, each two boys shouldering a pole with heavier luggage.

They marched all day, covering thirteen miles. With blistered feet they slept in a church in Dornstadt.

Formerly housing a population of several thousand, abandoned Dornstadt had not been heavily looted since the foot refugees from Munich had not yet arrived. The student group was like an army in the field now, an army living off the land. They made quick work of the market and few shops, focusing on food, soap, and toilet paper.

They each assembled a kit. Water bottles were fashioned from soda bottles, beer bottles with ceramic swing-top caps, and the like: one boy had a boda bag. The C-rations had left them with many minimalist can openers, but they picked up larger ones as well. Their plastic fork, spoon, and knife sets gave way to mismatched metal versions, along with pots, pans, and plates.

Being at the head of such an army, Josephine felt like Joan of Arc leading a children's crusade.

"Miss Wells?" It was Lea, one of the senior girls. "Uh, my shoes have given out, and I think some of the other kids have the same problem — can we get new shoes?"

"I guess we should. I guess we have to! Have you seen a shoe store nearby?"

"No, but there's a sporting goods store over there. Maybe they have boots."

The store was locked, and the students looked to Josephine with unease. She felt it, too. Taking food and food-related items had seemed necessary, but this seemed more like theft, even though it was also necessary. How many dozens of miles lay ahead?

She arrived at a solution.

"We will break in, but we will be tidy. We will take what we need and leave a note. After we get to France we can arrange to send money to pay for what we took."

The boys broke in through the glass door and about a dozen members of the party tried on boots. Even Josephine found a pair that fit. When it came time to leave, she was looking for a pen and paper, when bad-boy Emilio used spray paint on the big window, writing, "MUNICH AHS — MUSTANGS 9 BOOTS."

Josephine was torn. The painting looked like vandalism, but it told who had done it, indicating their intent to repay, and it would also act as a trail marker should anybody search for them. So she bit her tongue and nodded approval.

They marched on. They reached a point where they could leave the car-choked Highway 8 west toward Stuttgart by going either south across the plain to Ulm or north into the hills to Göppingen. Josephine did not have much choice, since Ulm was under attack.

They headed into the hills on the lesser-traveled road, still jammed with slow-moving cars. After they had hiked a few miles they saw an unusual thing: a vehicle heading east. It was a VW bus coming toward them, slowing as the hippies inside examined them. The driver leaned out and yelled, "Americans? You Americans?"

"Yes," cried Josephine. "We're Americans!"

"We help. Just the minute."

Josephine's heart swelled with hope and relief. A few tears ran down her cheeks as she thought of Todd.

The van idled on the other side of the road. The driver said, "Come over here, alone. Leave the kinder over there.

We have to talk with you in private."

She dodged around the slow moving cars, walking over to them. The driver waved her over to the shoulder, where one of the Germans in the back of the van shot her in the face, then in the chest. The vehicle sped off.

Senior football player Patrick and his brother Charlie ran out to Ms. Wells lying in the road. They tried all the first aid they could but she convulsed and died in their hands.

Now the students were on their own. Some of the younger girls began crying hysterically as blond Patrick and brunet Charlie carried the body over to their side of the road. Patrick said they had to calm down, and Charlie shouted for them to shut up. Senior Lea stepped in and said she would take care of it.

Class President Darren came over and demanded, "Why did they kill her?"

"I don't know," said Patrick, grinding his teeth. "I guess they were bad guys."

"But they —"

"We don't have time for this," snapped Patrick. "We don't have time to bury her. We have to get moving."

"Yes, I agree," said Darren. "I say we keep going to where Ms. Wells was leading us."

Patrick knelt down and took up the woman's purse. He opened it and started taking things out.

"Hey!" said Darren in outrage. "What're you doing?"

"I'm taking the map and anything else we need. Does anybody know where we're going?"

"I think it was 'Goppen,' something like that," said Charlie.

"Göppingen," said Darren's crony, the junior Brad.

"And then what?" asked Patrick. "I mean, where are we going? Paris?"

"Calais," said Brad. "Or Normandy. Someplace in Northern France."

"All right, then," said Patrick, his squinty eyes grim.

"Good to know."

They started hiking again.

After a while there was helicopter noise ahead, followed by gunships in the air. The kids scrambled for cover, ultimately lying down in the depression beside the road, and they saw the gunships race overhead on their way south.

The students resumed hiking.

Patrick was in front. Charlie caught up with him, and in a low voice asked him, "Who were those guys who killed Miss Wells?"

"I think they were commie gangsters, like the Baden-Meinkampf gang."

"Who?"

"You remember, a few years ago, those jerks running around killing people? There was that one rich guy killed out by Frankfurt, then the airplane was hijacked —"

"Yeah, yeah, I remember now. You think there's a lot of them around?"

"I hope not. I mean, most people are refugees now, right? So if we meet people who are not leaving, then maybe they are already working for the commies."

"We can't trust anyone."

"We have to be suspicious."

They hiked again for a while. Suddenly there was road noise ahead, and they ducked down on the roadside to watch as many US armored personnel carriers drove by at speed. The sight of these tank-like vehicles cheered them up. They were walking in the direction the APCs had come from, hoping to find a base where they would be welcome and safe.

Patrick looked at the map again.

"What's up?" asked Lea.

"I'm trying to figure where we are and how far we can go. Hey, thanks for taking care of the kids, before."

"Sure. Glad to help."

Even after a couple of days of camping, Lea looked pretty to Patrick, her curly light brown hair framing her elfin features. But he was mindful of their history: a year earlier they had gone on a date to see the movie "Grease," and he had been too fresh or something. She got mad at him, then she got a boyfriend whose family lived in town. That was Hector, another military brat, but a good friend of Patrick. Now presumably Hector was evacuating with his mom and siblings; his dad was fighting or dead, as were all of their dads.

Breaking out of these fleeting dark thoughts, he said, "You did good, as good as Miss Wells."

She looked away, like he had said something wrong, and said, "Can we get to the base tonight?"

"No. It must be twenty-five miles."

"Maybe we can get a ride with those soldiers when they come back," said Darren, working his way in.

Lea's face lit up with hope.

"That'll be great if it happens," said Patrick, "but we have to keep going. Looks like there's a castle ahead, maybe twelve miles."

"A castle!" said Ricky Gutierrez, seventh grader.

Indeed, after another long march they arrived at the ruins of Castle Helfenstein, located on a hill southeast of a town. Here they found a tower for shelter, along with toilets and water.

At the leadership meeting they talked of staying, of waiting out the war in this medieval spot. They knew they could not.

Ricky, who represented the thirteen remaining seventh-graders, said his group had decided the evacuation experience was like being on the Oregon Trail, and Patrick was the trail boss.

"It's also like a horror movie, you know?" said Ricky. "And the one thing about those movies is that the people all have to stay together. When they break up, bad things happen."

"Yeah," said Patrick, "we have strength in numbers." Most of the refugees they had seen were clumped in family groups of four or five; sometimes two families working together as ten. The students were ten times that size.

"I worry about my dad," said Ricky. "And my mom."

"We all worry about our folks," said Darren. "And I'm sure they worry about us. So we have to be brave, and keep on focus."

"Keep on marching," said Charlie.

"And stay together," said Ricky.

"Right," said Patrick. "Like a family."

Later, when the brothers were alone, Charlie got onto the topic of the killers again.

"I'd like to get them back for what they did," he said. "Kill them and take their guns, then we'd have guns."

"Jesus, Charlie, we've got to avoid trouble. If we had guns, the commies would shoot us on sight."

"Don't you want revenge?"

"Of course I do. But we can't risk everybody else. It's not like we're Robin Hood, we're on the Oregon Trail."

"Darren says we should turn ourselves over to the commies."

"You're kidding!"

"No."

"What the hell?"

"He thinks they will treat us okay."

"That's bullshit. That's total bullshit. Is he really saying that, or is he just talking?"

"I don't know. Maybe he's just talking."

"Well, I think the commies would kill us or put us in some horrible P.O.W. camp."

"Yeah."

"I guess we have to watch him, make sure he doesn't sell us out."

"Watch him like a movie — hey, we're not going to see *Avalanche Express*."

It was a welcome break in the tension. The two of them had been waiting over a year to see that action movie.

"I don't know," said Patrick. "Maybe we'll see it in France, or England."

"Remember Joe Namath last year? That was so cool, talking to him, and him telling about American football and now the movies he's doing . . ."

On the fifth morning of the war they came down from the hill and scavenged on their way through Geiselingen, a town whose population had numbered in the tens of thousands. A bunch of tanks went through, heading up toward Göppingen, but they looked like Soviet tanks.

At one point the Mustangs were spread out searching through a number of shops along a street, when Patrick heard a girl scream in the next building. He rushed over, tire iron at the ready, with Charlie unslinging his new baseball bat. They found a gang of five desperadoes dragging off a couple of struggling Mustang girls. The gang halted to fight off the brothers, but as more boys poured in, the Germans lost heart, let go of the girls, and fled.

The students hiked all day, only to discover that Cooke Barracks had been captured by Soviets. They spent the night in the woods.

At dawn they set out, following the train tracks to avoid Soviets on the roads. After about twelve miles they came to Plochingen, a town formerly housing several thousand. There was a Bosche factory located right next to the train station.

They went into the Bosche structure, hunting for the cafeteria. They found it, along with some vending machines that gave up candy bars and snacks to their tire irons and crowbars.

Patrick felt things were going well until he saw a red-faced Jennifer burst into the kitchen, making a beeline to her best friend Lea. Then Lea with a stormy brow brought it to him, that Emilio had tried to force himself on Jennifer, and what was Patrick going to do about it?

Emilio was a bad apple, a jerk, a loner who had somehow drifted into membership in the "President's

Council," the clique surrounding class president Darren.

Patrick and his brother Charlie had a private meeting with Emilio in a separate room.

"It's not like that," said Emilio with a sneer. "She led me on. She said things, did things. Then I guess she changed her mind, or maybe it was all a tease from the start, so I stopped."

"She had to fight you off."

"No. It's a case of 'he said, she said.' Wasn't there something like that with you and Lea last year? No harm, no foul. Besides, what are you going to do about it? I'm on the President's Council."

"You're on probation," said Patrick, menace shining from his squinty eyes. "Anything else like this and I'll beat the crap out of you."

"Oh yeah? You and what army?"

"Leadership group."

"Hey man, don't get all *Lord of the Flies* on me!"

"You're the one going outlaw on us."

•

Morning found the Mustangs following the railroad toward Stuttgart. From a distance the sky ahead had a dark smear, like the smog of a living city, but as they drew closer they saw black columns of smoke rising up from where fires were still burning in one area to the south. They made camp at the outskirts.

At sunrise Patrick was happy to see Lea coming over to see him, but then she gave him the bad news that a few students had diarrhea. That would slow down the whole group, or even force them to stop for a few days.

"Oh wow," said Patrick, dizzy at this new challenge. "So we've got to find a pharmacy? That's probably not so hard, but then we somehow find the right medicine, in German?"

"Wasn't there something the driver said about the C-ration peanut butter?"

"Yeah, using it for a cook fire."

"He also called it the best cure for the 'dirty squirties,'" she said, giving a wry smile.

"I guess I missed that!"

The pair asked around to find if anybody had a can of the stuff. There was only one, held by a ninth-grader named Preston, but he did not want to give it over for free, saying, "What's in it for me?"

Patrick was surprised by this. He suppressed his initial reaction of trying to pressure the kid on the common good, instead saying, "Good question. What can I offer you — money?"

"No, that's no good."

"What else is there, then?" asked Lea, her brow furrowed in puzzlement. "A favor?"

"No, too vague."

"What's this all about?" asked Patrick. "How come you held onto the can?"

"It's 'cause of the Jews."

"'The Jews'?" said Patrick, looking over to Lea, who shrugged.

"Yeah, see, they can't eat pork, you know? So they were in a bind with the C-rations — you heard how bad Ham and Lima Beans are, right?"

"Sure," said Patrick. To avoid giving the infamous nickname, he only said, "Legendary."

"Yeah. Well, while you were eating Spaghetti and Meatballs, or Chicken and Noodles, I was eating Ham and Lima Beans. It was awful."

"Okay, okay, I think I get it. You've already made sacrifices."

Preston nodded.

"But what do we have?" mused Lea.

"How about cigarettes?" said Patrick. "We're keeping them for trade, you know? So they're like money. I could give you some packs in trade for the peanut butter."

"How many?"

"Two."

"No way. Give me ten."

"Five."

"Make it seven, and they all have to be Marlboros. No menthols!"

•

On the eighth day they entered the ruins of Stuttgart. They chanced upon a market being looted by a squad of Soviet paratroopers using a civilian truck. Rashly, the Mustangs settled in to wait their turn, until the Soviet leader fired a warning shot in the air, which sent them in retreat.

Some miles later the Mustangs came upon a neighborhood that had been fortified, guarded by dour men with rifles and shotguns. Language proved to be a problem until Darren used Turkish.

"Where'd you learn Turkish?" asked Patrick, amazed.

"Turkey, duh," said Darren.

Patrick grinned sheepishly. Military brats lived in all sorts of places.

The Mustangs told the Turkish defenders about the Soviets they had seen at the market. The Turks nodded at that. The Mustangs asked if there were Americans nearby. The Turks said no: a nuke had hit Kelley Barracks, about four miles to the south, and all the other Americans went west. They told them that France was still neutral and thus a safe haven for them was just across the border. The Turks were proud to be fighting the Russians again.

The Mustangs asked about food, since the locations over the last few miles had been already picked clean. The Turks generously offered them all the pork products they could carry, and they offered to barter kosher items for cigarettes.

Once the trading was done, the Mustangs headed southwest toward Patch American High School. Their path cut across the outer edge of destruction from the Kelley nuke. Wood-framed buildings were collapsed, or leaned drunkenly. Brick apartment buildings showed signs of severe damage. Trees and utility poles had been knocked down, all in the same direction. There were lots of ruined cars, some on the street as if parked there, others thrown in from the east.

They found a damaged cinema to camp in.

The next noon they found Patch American High School, close to Highway 8. The brand new school was burned out, with no help for them except for a message spray-painted on the front door: "Evac Karlsruhe." Emilio sprayed "Mustangs" next to it.

On day ten they set out on Highway 8 again, this time toward Karlsruhe, a distance of about forty-five miles. It rained off and on, making things more miserable. Some of the girls started singing songs from "Grease," mainly "You're the One That I Want" and "Summer Nights." The morale boosting was infectious, and most of the Mustangs joined in. The boys and girls sang their parts of idyllic "Summer Nights" in a call and response that temporarily lifted them all out of their grim situation. Then Patrick led them in the Mustang fight song.

They camped near Rutesheim that night, then hiked off the highway through forest and past farms to reach the town of Pforzheim the next night, on the northern edge of the Black Forest. They gave a big push on day twelve, marching along a forest road in order to arrive at Karlsruhe in late afternoon.

The Mustangs found a city sparsely inhabited by soldiers and civilian defenders, all of them quick on directions. A soldier told them to go to Paul Revere Village, at 11 o'clock off the traffic circle. At the Village a priest told them to go to Gerszewski Barracks to the west. At the gate to "the Zoo," the guards directed them to a tent city several blocks west. This refugee stop was built on a soccer field northeast of a cul-de-sac neighborhood of houses.

57

Class President Darren spoke to the officers in charge of the tents, and he came back with a good news/bad news situation. The good news was that a convoy was setting out for France within minutes. The bad news was that there was only enough room for half the students.

"We could send the seventh and eighth graders," said Lea.

"That's about thirty-five," said Brad.

"Add the ninth graders," said Darren.

"You can go with them," quipped Charlie.

"Hell no!"

"No," said Patrick. "Send all the girls and the seventh grade boys."

"What are you saying?" snapped Lea. "You saying girls can't handle it?"

"I'm saying that's the way to do it. The best way."

"I won't go. I'm staying with you."

"We need you to go. You're like Miss Wells. Those little kids, they need you."

She looked away, squinting as she wrestled with it. Finally she gave a sigh of resignation and said, "Rickie's going to hate it, breaking up the Mustangs."

"We'll get the next bus out," said Darren. "Like, tomorrow." The boys nodded. "We'll all meet up soon."

Once the convoy was away, the President's Council stayed inside the tent city, while the rest of the Mustangs camped outside, on a grassy island with trees in the cul-de-sac.

"We made it," said Charlie after a dinner of C-rations. "I can't believe how far we walked."

"Long ways," admitted Patrick with a haunted smile. He was worried about the fate of those on the bus. Would the bus survive the trip? How long would it take? What if something bad happened? He was worried about Lea. What if she met up with Hector again at the refugee camp?

Patrick snorted a laugh at himself. If Lea and Hector survived, that was good and good. So why did it feel bad?

58

A figure came between the tents, headed toward them.

"Emilio," muttered Charlie.

When the boy was close enough for conversation, Patrick said, "What's up?"

"I agree with you. I want to stay out here."

"Suit yourself," said Patrick, figuring he had been sent as a spy.

Early the next morning, Brad came over to invite the Mustangs in for breakfast.

"Come on, guys," he said. "A good hot meal."

"No," said Patrick, eyeing the tents a hundred meters away. "We'll go scavenging."

"But why?"

"That's what we do." He knew he was dodging the question, so he took it straight on. "The base isn't safe, it's a target. Remember Cooke Barracks."

"The war is winding down, that's what they say."

Emilio chuffed and said, "Watch out for 'Armistice Day.'"

"Why are we even here?" said Charlie. "We could walk to France in an hour."

"We'll get a ride soon, and that's better than walking," said Brad. "So don't wander too far, okay?"

"Yeah," said Patrick. "See you later."

The scavenging was pretty poor until the Mustangs found a local store being run like a frontier trading post. Here they bartered the last of their cigarette packs for food.

They returned to their camp under the trees, ate their food, and waited. Hours went by. Army trucks rolled past them to park next to the soccer field. More time crawled by. The Mustangs got up and began pacing around.

Patrick knew he could not hold them back much longer when he saw Brad walking toward them on the path between the tents. Charlie saw him, too, and looked over at Patrick. Patrick sighed, picked up his daypack, and started walking toward the tents, with the rest following his lead.

As Brad walked out past the last tents there was a line in the air to the east, a rocket that exploded in such a muted way it seemed like a dud. But an alarm went off on the base, and the President's Council was running for the cul-de-sac. The Mustangs had come to a full stop on the road, watching with horror as Brad ran toward them. Soldiers were dashing around the trucks, and some of them fell over in convulsions.

The Mustangs turned and ran away. Patrick looked back and saw Brad still following, but Darren and the others had fallen. Now the soldiers running around had gas masks on.

The Mustangs kept running. Some of the boys had dropped their kits as they ran.

"Wait!" cried Brad, running hard, trying to catch up.

Nobody answered. All kept running.

After about 140 yards they reached a highway. Patrick dropped back.

"Stop!" he shouted at Brad, holding his arms up.

Brad, lugging two kits he had picked up on the fly, stopped and doubled over, heaving deep gasps.

"Stay there," said Patrick. "Keep your distance."

The other boys stopped at the highway, fanned out.

"What the hell!" said Brad. "Why?"

"We don't know what it is," said Patrick. "And we don't want to get it."

"What?! They're dead, man! They're dead!"

"I know. How do you feel?"

"Me? I feel sick," said Brad, as Charlie came to stand beside his brother Patrick.

"What kind of sick?"

"'Seeing my friends die' kind of sick."

"What do you think?" asked Charlie in quiet tones. "Biological, or chemical?"

"No idea," said Patrick. "Doesn't matter." He called out to Brad, "Look, just keep a distance between us for a while, you know?"

"Yeah, yeah. I get it. Makes sense. I'll carry these packs like a mule until we see if I got cooties. So what now?"

"We're walking to France."

•

The highway was a return to the traffic jam scene of the first days. It took them about an hour to get to the bridge across the Rhine. There were forty-seven of them, Brad having been allowed back in when soldiers told them the Zoo attack had been chemical.

The other side of the border was another traffic jam. The only difference was that in France it was a refugee crisis.

The Mustangs were steered south to a camp near Lauterbourg. The place was hard used and squalid for being only ten days old — the Stuttgart walkers had begun arriving a week earlier. The German refugees were haunted and sullen. A few blowhards went so far as to blame the war on the students, but the Americans had safety in their numbers and the improvised weapons ready in their fists.

There were no buses waiting for them, and the train was no help since it only ran north or south into West Germany. These details were dispiriting because the Mustangs had been focused on getting to France, but they had to press on. The new goal was to get to Metz, a city about 100 miles away.

The next day they hiked to Betschdorf, a town that looked disturbingly German with its half-timber buildings. The day after that, they logged another fifteen miles to Zinswiller. Here they discovered they were close to some castle ruins, and so on Day Sixteen they went five miles off the refugee track to visit Chateau de Lichtenberg.

The Mustangs went up narrow roads and trail shortcuts, always uphill, until at last they arrived at the top.

They found an open shell of a guardhouse next to a bridge over a dry moat. Crossing this, they entered a half pipe tunnel, angled to the right, going up. They emerged on the plateau, surrounded by ruins of a chapel, two towers with a shield wall between them, and other structures.

The place was much bigger than the previous castle they had visited, but it had never been restored. The effects of a final war had remained unrepaired, and the passage of centuries had added further deterioration. It was very sobering to the boys, having just come from a hot war, to see the cold ruins from another age.

Patrick went over to the western edge of the rampart and saw the village spread out below. There was a church in the middle and another church spire close up, visible behind trees on the slope below the castle moat.

Patrick heard a rumble of yelling men from somewhere down there, behind the trees, and then the sound of a gunshot. A girl's scream.

"What the hell?" said Charlie. "This is France!"

"What's going on?" said Brad.

"Let's find out," said Patrick.

There was no fast way down: the Mustangs had to jog back across the plateau and down to the bridge. From the guardhouse they followed the narrow brick road to the left, coming around the hill in a counter-clockwise manner. They hurried around the curve and the road straightened in the direction of the village. They passed trees on the slope to the left and a few cottages on the right, then they saw space open up ahead, with a long, two-story building on the left before a traffic circle.

Patrick led the way, keeping close to the long building. He shrugged off his pack and crept up on the corner, tire iron in his hand.

From the corner, the road stretched another twenty-four yards to the roundabout. At the center of the circle, about twelve yards in, stood a man in paramilitary garb. This leader was giving a stern lecture to a captive audience of old men at the other side of the circle, villagers cowed by a line of five paramilitaries with rifles and shotguns who faced them.

An old stone church faced the circle, at about 2 o'clock. On the steps of the church two paramilitaries knelt in holding down a teenage girl, while a third lowered himself on top of her writhing form.

It looked bad, but the Mustangs were "backstage" to the theatrics, and thus they had complete surprise. Patrick turned to the others, noting with satisfaction that they had already ditched their packs and readied their weapons. But before he could begin to whisper a plan, the girl screamed, and Charlie beside him was off like a shot, charging straight in.

There was no time for thinking: Patrick launched himself after his brother.

Patrick followed Charlie for five seconds, until the younger boy hit the circle and dogged right, aiming for the rape team. Patrick could hear the footfalls behind him, the charging of the Mustangs. To save his brother he had to go straight on and take out that lecturing leader.

All his football training snapped into place, fueled by his fury for the paramilitaries who had killed Miss Wells. He sprinted toward the leader, gaining speed.

The captive crowd gasped in surprise, causing some of their guards to glance around toward their leader. The leader also glanced back, and his bearded face did a double take. Patrick raced closer. The leader turned around, fumbled at his holster.

From somewhere behind Patrick came the solid thunk of baseball bat against bone, very satisfying. Close behind him was a yell of many voices.

The leader drew his pistol as he took two steps back, like a quarterback setting up to snap a pass. Patrick lowered his shoulder and continued his charge.

The pistol was coming down to point at him.

A rifle went off by the crowd.

And then Patrick piled into the man's solar plexus with all the force of a full, hard, dirty tackle . . .

•

Lea was strung out from the strain. She and the first evacuation group had been at the camp in Calais for a week. The other half of the group should have arrived the next day, or the day after that. Every time a bus or truck arrived at one of the three gates, she rushed through the tent city of the camp to meet her friends, only to find that all the newcomers were strangers. Day after day, crushing the kids down, until now they were all just lying around.

Reclining upon a makeshift sleeping pad, Lea worried about her mother and her little brother, wondering if they had made it out to Italy. She figured that her father was dead, but she prayed he was not. She felt a flash of anger at Patrick: Where was he? He had said the boys would come on the next bus!

Then she was confused at thinking of Patrick like he was her boyfriend. What about Hector? She groaned with guilt and shame at having neglected thinking of Hector, but he was in the same maddening category as her mother and brother, whereas she had tramped across burning West Germany with Patrick and the others for two weeks. They had pulled together, driving the kids along, and through his actions Patrick had proven to be strong and fair. She was fond of him, which alarmed her, so she reminded herself of his pawing behavior that one time before. This did not dissolve her feeling, or even dent it.

She told herself she was anxious about all of them: Charlie, Darren, Brad, even Emilio. And the rest of them, including Patrick.

She heard a faint calling, but then in the humming quiet she knew it must be a dream she had just woken from.

She heard it again. Voices off in the distance, shouting one word. Her heart surged.

She sat up. Jennifer was looking at her in stark amazement, saying, "Did you hear — ?"

"Mustangs!" she shouted. She stood and raced out of

the tent. "Mustangs!"

"Mustangs," came the answering call, while around her girls burst forth from their tents.

Now all the girls shouted, "Mustangs!"

It was like a game of Marco Polo, and the boys were getting closer with each cry.

"Mustangs!"

"Mustangs!" shouted Lea, and then she saw Patrick's face in the crowd. She ran toward him, fighting through the stream, tears pouring out of her eyes and her throat suddenly too choked up to shout. In an uncertain world where one or both parents might be dead, and where West Germany might be lost, she found herself reunited with a group of people who meant the world to her.

ATOMIC MISSIONS

1. Operation Olympic

"Where were you the day the first atomic bombs were dropped?" Pierce asked Buddy Dutchman.

They were at a seedy cantina on the beach, a few miles away from San Diego. It was sunset at the end of a hot day. Pierce and Granberry were wearing sombreros and drinking bottles of beer, sitting on a bench surrounded by Mexican peasants all betting on the fighting roosters in the ring.

"Miyazaki," said Buddy.

"The first will always be remembered," said Granberry.

Winslow and the other four were all watching the sunset intently, swearing and saying cockfight-things like "Look at him go!" and "Get 'em." The eight Anglos were using their old flash goggles as sunglasses.

"I dunno, it's all a part of X-Day," said Buddy.

"Still, our one bomb put a dent in those three Jap divisions, I'll betcha," said Granberry.

Empty bottles lay on the ground and the hollow remains of a piñata dangled from a beam.

The sunset was getting brighter. Buddy thought, *It's strange, like a film running backwards or the sun rising in the west.*

Probably just one of those optical illusions right at sunset where the sun splits in two with a green flash.

"I taste lead," said Pierce, looking askance at the bottle in his hand. "You taste lead?"

The beach reminded Buddy of Miyazaki. He wondered what it had been like for those Japanese soldiers, guarding the beach against the landing force on the horizon. The odds had been three to two in favor of the Allies, but a successful invasion required odds of at least three to one. Buddy figured the Japanese soldiers had felt confident and ready, seeing better odds than the Germans had faced at D-Day, six months earlier. It was a classic strategic scenario, and by the numbers revealed they could see that the Allies did not have the strength left to enter the endgame on the proper footing. But then the fire had hit the beach out of the blue sky, and the odds were changed in an instant.

It was funny and it was sickening. Buddy wanted to get off the beach and walk down the road to take shelter in the safety of a population center.

"Where you going?" said Winslow to Buddy.

"Stretch my legs," said Buddy.

"Good idea. It's a long trip back."

He walked into the cantina and found himself inside a log cabin. On the wall was a collection of tools: a pickaxe, a shovel, and a placer pan for fishing gold out of the American River. There was a big new radio like the kind he had at home, its wooden face like a cathedral. There was a table with a few smaller radios, a vacuum flask, eight metal coffee cups, and a map of Japan. Buddy looked over his shoulder and through the open doorway he saw the Sutter's Mill replica. He was in Coloma, the Sierra foothills town where gold was discovered in 1849: Ground Zero of the Gold Rush.

A science fiction serial was softly coming from the radio: ". . . thirty megaton thermonuclear warhead! That's a city-buster!"

Buddy snickered at such gobbledygook. *That Buck Rogers stuff is always like that, pushing things to absurd levels, jamming "scientific" words together into gibberish like "megaton" and "thermonuclear."*

"And now, in one stroke, I'll remove all obstacles from my path and take my rightful place as master of the world!"

He turned down the volume and caught the beginning of a song coming from one of the other radios: "*I'm as restless as a willow in a windstorm . . .*"

At the back of the cabin there was a trapdoor in the dirt floor and a half-door in the wall. The half-door was high up, like the upper half of a Dutch door.

He went up the short stepladder and through the back door, looking for a toilet or an outhouse, but found himself sitting in a little boat floating in a Tunnel of Love ride at the Long Beach Pike, cool in the dark, shaded from the hot California sun. Sitting next to him was Dee Dee Mc-Teague, looking both prim and alluring in her WASP uniform. Everybody at the B-29 field at Windover, Nevada had thought that the new bomber was too dangerous to use, and it was, but then Dee Dee had flown "Lady Bird" in, shaming them into it. Buddy didn't have his arm around her yet.

"*Keep your hands in the boat,*" said a recorded voice. "*Don't rock the boat.*"

The scene on the right bank was a romantic one of a lady and her knight. Dee Dee gave a sigh of pleasure, and Buddy, leaning over, caught a whiff of her cotton-candy breath.

"It's all about chivalry and codes of war," murmured Buddy.

"It's Romance," said Dee Dee.

"And we live in Romantic times," said Buddy, putting his arm around her. "Just like them."

"How so, good knight?"

"Population centers are like the old castles. We can lay

siege to them but we cannot target non-combatants. All fighting is between professional soldiers."

"And the peasants who get in the way," said Dee Dee.

"Like in olden times, I guess."

"*Keep your hands in the boat,*" droned the recording. "*Don't rock the boat.*"

He twisted around to kiss her in the awkward confines of the boat, but she turned her face away, so he felt for the step with his foot.

He found it and climbed down into the card room from the ventilation duct, closing the grille behind him. The three gunners sat around a green felt table, smoking cigarettes and playing poker.

"Hey, it's the bombardier," said Tuller. "The Man of the Hour."

"How's it look up there?" said Eastman.

"Did you hit your mark?" said Yeldham.

"Yeah, I think so," said Buddy. "But as you could see, I might have been off by a thousand feet and it would hardly matter."

"Yeah, that was sure something all right," said Eastman. "Now just the long flight back."

"You want to play a few hands?" said Yeldham.

"Naw," said Buddy. "I'm just heading for the can."

"Suit yourself," said Tuller.

Leaving the plush card room, Buddy entered the tiny lavatory of the B-29 bomber. In the claustrophobic confines he lowered his pants, sat on the toilet, and dropped a load.

He rested his chin on his fists. With his eyes closed it was almost an attitude of prayer. He was relieved that the mission objective had been completed: six bombers had each dropped a bomb, three on the beachheads and three on the inland reserves. He was thankful *Luke the Spook* hadn't been shot down yet. Six magic pumpkins planted, a sudden mushroom forest sprouted, towering over Southern Kyushu. The Allied troops would land on Miyazaki's blasted beach in an hour. He was hoping that the war would come to an abrupt end now, so they could be home for Christmas. That goal had seemed more likely before the October typhoon had set everything back a month.

When he opened his eyes again he was at the bombsight in the nose of the plane.

2. Operation Coronet

The Plexiglas nose cone made Buddy think of a round cathedral window with all the leading and the glass. A stained-glass picture of blue sky above and tan earth below, the view from a cloud.

He shook himself.

No time for daydreaming or thinking about last time.

The tail-gunner had been singing over the intercom early in the flight, and now in the silence of the bomb-run the song ran through Buddy's head: *Zip-a-dee-doo-dah, zip-a-dee-ay.*

Through the bombsight Buddy looked down on rice paddies about fifty miles northwest of Tokyo. It was 1 March 1946, and their objective was to soften up the interior for the invasion of Tokyo Bay. Others from the 509th Composite Group were nuking the beaches in preparation for the largest amphibious assault in history — four times the size of the Normandy Invasion — using American, British, and Australian forces. Just like they had done in Southern Kyushu three months before.

My oh my what a wonderful day.

Ota was a rural town with a factory building fighter planes, a railroad connecting the prefectural capital to Tokyo, and some troop concentrations on the south side. The place had been hit several times with conventional bombs — a B-29 or three had even gone down in the area — but that was the old way.

Plenty of sunshine headin' their *way.*

Buddy released his atom bomb on the bulls-eye, between the railroad and the Imperial Army, two miles outside of city limits. As the bomb fell away, the bomber made its customary sharp turn for the flight back to Miyazaki.

Buddy closed his eyes as he put on his flash goggles. When he opened his eyes it was dark. Too dark. He lifted the goggles for a peek and found it was night.

3. Operation Hudson Harbor

What the hell? thought Buddy, startled. *It seems like I've been on this plane for days, forever. Why did I have my goggles on already? Just to see what I could see — yes, that's right, an experiment.*

It was a night flight in the moonless dark of 6 April 1951. An atomic armada of forty B-29s filled the air on their way to bomb all the Red Chinese airbases and depots strung across the Manchurian side of the Korean Peninsula, from Antung in the west to Hunchun in the east.

The area near Antung had been known as "MiG Alley" ever since some B-29s dropping iron bombs had been surprised by the first Soviet-made MiG jet fighters in Korea. That was in November, five months ago.

Buddy was at his station in the nose of *Luke the Spook*, looking out into the darkness as they entered MiG Alley. He thought about the mission:

First nukes for the U.N. If we can get the Chicom and the Soviets out of here, then we can be home for Christmas. The Chicom can't nuke, but if the Soviets want to fly a bomber over to nuke an airbase in Alaska, they can try. And they know what they'll get in response — they've only got around forty bombs, and we're using that amount right here, right now.

There were a few shudders through the bomber, an explosion, and Buddy saw the fiery tail of a MiG swoop down in front.

The bail bell rang. Buddy fumbled into his parachute harness and grabbed the precious bombsight while the other airmen shouted and scrambled. When he opened the bombardier escape hatch he was sucked out into the blackness at 30,000 feet.

We're dead, he thought. *My God, we're dead when our pumpkin goes.*

Even through this sense of doom he counted out the seconds for a long fall.

Could Remington have gone in there to disarm it after the bail bell rang? Sacrificing himself to give the rest of us a chance? Gone in there with an air mask and his tool kit, opening up the bomb and pulling out the trigger?

With a jerk Buddy was floating in the quiet. He strained to see the stricken bomber, still counting the seconds since he had jumped. He wondered how far away from the atomic blast he would have to be to survive in the air, with a fragile silk parachute.

Eight miles for the plane to survive, so maybe twenty miles for me in the open? That would be how many seconds at our last speed?

He closed his eyes in concentration. *Two hundred thirty miles per hour is about four miles a minute, so I need five minutes* and saw light through his eyelids.

Here it comes! He instinctively opened his eyes.

It was like a dream. He was floating down on a beautiful, clear day, and all of Japan was out there before him, Mount Fuji near the horizon.

What was that? I must've blacked out from the pressure change. It's Y-Day.

Buddy looked around for the mushroom clouds but there weren't any to be seen. He looked south to Tokyo Bay where the amphibious landings would be happening, but the bay's shape and orientation were wrong.

It's funny how Tokyo Bay is a miniature version of the Yellow Sea, where the Boso Peninsula sticks out like Korea. But this one looks more like the San Francisco Bay than either of those.

What he had taken for Mount Fuji was Mount Shasta of California. He drifted down to Sonoma.

No, it's not Y-Day. Luke the Spook, *my old bomber, was shot down over Korea. I thought I was going to die. Maybe I did? It's just a memory brought on by being in a parachute again, revisiting that trauma. The war's over — Korea is free.*

There was a crowd seated on bleachers on the plaza before the Spanish Mission, where some American adventurers had just replaced the Mexican flag with a bear flag of their own design when Buddy landed in the plaza. The spectators gasped and cheered. Children ran to touch the silk.

The band played. A politician gave a short speech about the town, calling it the meeting place of two worlds.

"The last Spanish mission was built here, 700 miles up the Camino Real from the first one in San Diego. And here the bear flag was first raised, marking the birth of the Republic of California!"

Afterwards Buddy toured the mission and found they were working at restoring it. "Here in the garden we are building a monument of clear glass blocks," said Simonson, the man leading the tour. "It is a miniature of the Mission, to serve as a memorial to Hiroshima, Nagasaki, Kokura, and Niigata."

"Why those cities?" asked Buddy.

"The Bomb," said Simonson.

Buddy shrugged. "Sure they were bombed, a lot of Jap cities were bombed."

"*Atomic* bomb."

"What are you trying to pull?" said Buddy, scoffing. "Is this some kind of Commie prank? No cities have been nuked!"

"Now look here —"

"No, you look!" said Buddy. "I was there — I dropped the bomb at Miyazaki, at Ota —"

"What are you talking about? Where's Miyasaki?"

Buddy wanted to punch Simonson in the face but instead he turned and stormed away into the church. He sat at a pew, closed his eyes, and tried to ease the rage in his heart.

When he opened his eyes again he was at the bombsight in the nose of another plane.

4. Operation Vulture

Buddy felt a chill run up his back.

It seems like I've been on this plane for days, but we just took off. Took off without an engine fire — that's it, I'm just relieved. Mind plays little tricks under the pressure.

They were fifteen minutes out from Miyazaki heading west, so it was the time to arm the bomb. Buddy heard them talking about it over the intercom and found himself curious about the arming process, or more precisely the e-mergency disarming process.

"Mind if I watch?" he asked.

"No, not at all," said Redford. "Come on."

Buddy left *Necessary Evil*'s bombardier station, walked away from the cockfight (this time behind a meat packing plant within sight of Mission San Gabriel in Los Angeles), and entered the Sierra cabin. Warton was sitting at the table, marking up a map of Southeast Asia, and Nichols stood beside him. Buddy went down the trap door this time and stepped out into the heat and humidity of an Indian spring.

They were on a dock, with cargo ships at berths all around them. The bomb was hanging horizontally from a scaffold, reminding Buddy of the log used to ring a temple bell in Japan at the Slag Buddha of Kamakura. It was as big as a trashcan, and Redford was underneath it like a mechanic working on a car.

"Welcome to the bomb bay," said Redford. "Here we go again, huh? Seems like every couple or three years we got another pumpkin run."

"Yeah."

It was 6 April 1953, and the mission was to relieve the French at the siege of Dien Bien Phu. A very small scale operation, using only three B-29s to drop three bombs in Northern Vietnam, it would be the first "surgical strike."

On the mat next to Redford were tools, bomb plates, and a pumpkin core.

"*Oh life could be a dream, sh-boom,*" sang Redford.

"I don't know about that 'boom' part," said Buddy.

Redford groaned.

"He ain't alive for a while yet," said Redford. "'Peter, Peter, pumpkin eater, had a wife and couldn't keep her,'" he chanted as he worked the wrench. "'Put her in a pumpkin shell . . . and there he kept her very well.'" He put the wrench down. "Hand me that core, will you?"

"This must be the wife, then," said Buddy, giving him the cylinder.

"Yup, you got it."

"You know, I was in Bombay back in April of '44."

"Yeah?"

"It was a big staging ground for X-Day."

"You don't say," said Redford.

Buddy looked up at the English cargo ship beside them at berth number one, read the name painted on her side: *Fort Stikine*.

"There was a cargo ship, the *Fort Stikine* — we were joking that it should be called 'Fort Stinking' because it had a ripe cargo of fish manure, but it also had fourteen hundred tons of munitions."

The stevedores had quit for lunch. After they left there was a wisp of smoke from the cargo hold, as if the cargo was taking a break, too, and having a few cigarettes.

"At four o'clock I was walking around, looking for a place to get a beer," said Buddy. "I must've been a half-mile from the docks — I could tell they were fighting a fire down by the water but it seemed pretty minor.

"I was asking this English officer for directions when there was a huge explosion — and I mean huge, it was nearly atomic. All the windows around us were blown out, and when I looked down at the dock I couldn't see anything but a big cloud of smoke covering the whole area.

"That was all in a second or less. I turned to the guy beside me and he wasn't there anymore. I looked around and his legs were over here and his upper body was over there. He'd been cut in half by a piece of metal plate."

Buddy had tried putting the Englishman back together, then he got sick for a while.

"It was a mess, with the blood and the fire, and smoke, and the choking stink of fish manure everywhere. People were screaming and running around. Some were saying it was Pearl Harbor again, that the Japs were attacking the ships. I tried to help people in the area.

"That's when the second explosion came, and it really was a mushroom cloud — the ship itself went a thousand feet straight up, on a pillar of smoke. Everybody ran for cover and all the metal bits came down like hail, killing more."

Redford came out from under the bomb, saying, "A little pumpkin for the Viet Minh."

"So it is pretty complicated to arm it —" said Buddy.

"Not much to it."

"But if we had to ditch . . ."

"Don't worry about it," said Redford.

"It's just —"

"I know, I know," said Redford. "You're just spooked about *Luke*."

"Well, yeah."

"But it didn't go off, *did* it?" asked Redford. He struck a pose and sang in his Dean Martin voice: "*When you walk in a dream but you know you're not dreaming, signore, 'scusa me, but you see, back in old Napoli, that's* amore."

Buddy went up from India into the miner's cabin, then into the Tunnel of Love. He was with Dee Dee again, and a new scene appeared on the left: a group of women with bamboo spears killing a downed airman.

"Scary," said Buddy.

"Yes," said Dee Dee, huddling close.

The women were Japanese, with disheveled hair and tattered kimono. Their eyes were wide in their dust-streaked faces, their mouths twisted in savage grimaces.

"*Keep your hands in the boat.*"

"I thought the tunnel ride was supposed to be either

scary or romantic," said Buddy.

"Now it's both," said Dee Dee. "Super modern."

On the horizon behind the amazons was a mushroom cloud, painted in Halloween colors of orange and black. The supine airman had two spears stuck in his gut. A scattering of spent brass casings showed his resistance, but the pistol's slide was locked open, revealing he was out of ammunition.

"They blur the line between non-combatant and soldier," said Dee Dee. "That's what makes it scary."

"When they take up weapons they become combatants," said Buddy.

"They were told they would be raped and murdered," said Dee Dee. "They fight to defend themselves."

"They are still combatants."

"*Don't rock the boat.*"

"They were fierce," said Dee Dee. "That there are any Japanese left is a miracle."

"Yeah. There aren't enough to run the place, though. Indians in the British sector, Koreans in the American sector, and Germans in the Russian sector."

She kissed him hungrily, her slim tongue spiraling around his own. It was a little frightening, but he closed his eyes, relaxed, and tried to enjoy it, even though there was a sudden stitch in his side.

"Wake up, Buddy," said a man's voice. "No time for napping."

Buddy opened his eyes. He was sitting in a chair in the wait room of a Stateside bomber field.

5. Operation Pluto

"Rough night last night?" asked Wolcott.

"No," said Buddy, finding his voice. "Smooth . . . tunnel of love."

Through the window Buddy could see their "Buff" being loaded up: the crew installed the plutonium bombs into the belly of the B-52 using the latest motorized gear, a far cry from the atomic pits at Okinawa and Miyazaki.

"You dog," said Wolcott with a leer. "You want some pep pills?"

"Yeah, sure," said Buddy. "Give me a couple."

The Buff was ready. The six airmen walked out to it.

"'*Cause I'm the wanderer — yeah, the wanderer*," sang Buddy. "*I roam around around around.*"

"That should be your theme song, Buddy," said Wolcott. "You're like the Flying Dutchman."

Buddy gave a laughing huff. The weather was comfortably warm and humid, a typical October morning in Louisiana.

"And you," said Buddy, "you're the Duke of Earl."

The job in front of them was a dream case of nukes-at-sea. Pure military, with no possibility of fallout on civilians: the interception of a Soviet ship carrying atom bombs to Cuba. Navy had wanted to do it, naturally, but they had the blockade to deal with.

The airmen climbed in and took their places on upper and lower flight decks. The cockpit was in the ruins of Mission San Luis Obispo this time, and the unbroken piñata swayed in the breeze. There was no Plexiglas nose-cone on a B-52, no windows on the lower deck, just the banks of machinery and radar screens in a crypt beneath the church. Buddy sat at the radar/bombardier station, with Wolcott at the radar navigator station beside him.

Before long the eight Pratt & Whitney turbojet engines were moving them down the runway. Buddy was tense, but reminded himself that this wasn't a B-29 with engines that would sometimes catch fire on takeoff. Still, he closed his eyes and said a little prayer for their safety.

"You okay, Buddy?" asked Simonson.

Buddy opened his eyes. He was back at Mission Sonoma, meeting place of two worlds. He turned in the pew and looked Simonson straight in the eye.

"I don't believe in your four radioactive cities, or in your Godzilla, your giant ants, your ICBMs, or your megatons."

"It would be a better world if there were no atomic bombs," said Simonson.

"I'm sure some people said the same thing about the first cannon, the first musket," said Buddy. "You can't put the genie back in the bottle, you can't outlaw the new weapon."

"Poison gas was outlawed," said Simonson. "So were fléchettes."

"But those are in a different category," said Buddy. "Gas is indiscriminate, unguided, just like the Nazi rocket bombs. And fléchettes were designed to maim and wound."

"If you could change anything, what would it be?"

"I'd find out about Bombay," said Buddy. "Maybe that fire could have been avoided, and that materiel would've helped the invasion, made the war end sooner."

"How about ending the war a year earlier by nuking a few population centers?" said Simonson. "Miyazaki had a population of a couple hundred thousand, right? And you say you bombed that."

"The cut off for a population center was two hundred thousand, and Miyazaki only had one-sixty," said Buddy. "But it was a known battlefield — the Japs knew we were coming there."

"Still, you say three towns were bombed that day," said Simonson. "If each one was half the size of Hiroshima, that still adds up to one and a half Hiroshimas."

"It wouldn't work and it is too barbaric to consider," said Buddy. "Firebombing Tokyo and Dresden, that was bad enough. Why do something even worse?"

"It sends a message."

"You want to send a message, use a telegram."

"You okay, Buddy?"

"I bombed a cathedral in Germany," said Buddy. "An iron bomb, before we had nukes. That's what I hate about the old way, bombing targets in cities, with flak popping all around and enemy fighters swarming like hornets. I made a mistake — I dropped too early, and ruined a medieval church.

"That's why I'm working here at the Mission, to atone for that. I don't believe in your four radioactive cities. It's all an insane dream, your Nazi missiles with super-atomic warheads, all of them pointing at population centers. Generations living with guilt and the fear of apocalypse coming at any moment."

Buddy closed his eyes. "In my heart the memorial is for Tokyo, Dresden, and Hamburg. As I build it, when I put those glass blocks into place, I think of them."

He opened his eyes. He was at his station in the Buff and he had just nuked Germany.

6. German Reunification

"Where were you the day the first neutron bombs were dropped?" Palmer asked Buddy.

They were in the cemetery at Mission Dolores, safe in the bosom of San Francisco. It was sunset at the end of a hot day: Palmer and Godfrey were wearing sombreros and drinking bottles of beer, sitting on a bench in front of the ring. They were surrounded by a busload of tourists: Japanese, Chinese, Russians, Vietnamese, and Russian sailors with their white hats. All of them were betting on the fighting roosters in the ring.

"Fulda Gap," said Buddy.

"The first will always be remembered," said Godfrey.

The three Americans were using their flash goggles as sunglasses.

"I dunno, it's all a part of the Big One," said Buddy.

"Still, our one bomb put a dent in those Russky divisions, I'll betcha."

"*It's the end of the world as we know it,*" sang Godfrey. "*And I feel fine.*"

Empty bottles lay on the ground and the hollow remains of a piñata dangled from a beam.

"Where you going?"

"Use the can," said Buddy.

"Good idea. It's a long trip back to Lakenheath."

The sunset was getting brighter. Buddy thought, *It's strange, like a film running backwards or the sun rising in the west. Probably just one of those optical illusions right at sunset where the sun splits in two with a green flash.*

SCOUT TEAM FROM THE ARC

Once there was an association of scientists who were so concerned about the future that they retreated into a secret base beneath Mount Whitney, where they would weather the collapse with a large number of nubile interns. Cut off from the world in this academic-industrial arcology, they formed plans and ran simulations on how to restore technological civilization to a fallen America, beginning in the California desert near Nevada.

After twenty-four years of isolation, the Arc leadership decided to send out the first scout team. A committee awarded the job to four young members, selected to be non-threatening. Team-leader Albert, a notorious deal-maker, was small-framed. Carl, a competent engineer, was black. Dim, heavy-set Maxine was chosen as the security officer in the belief that the "neobarbarians" would be patriarchal and thus not see her as a fighter. Sivlo, the medic, was a gengineered chimp-man.

Albert and his team set out from the subterranean Arcology in a white armored car. Their task was to make contact with a settlement of neobarbarians, the opening move of the Arc's Mission.

Carl drove the car down from the eastern Sierra Nevada, heading toward the former truck-stop hamlet of Lone Pine in the high desert. Emerging from the yellow pine forest they found a landscape increasingly changed from what was on their old map. In the foothills they discovered a forest of structures Carl identified as wind turbines, but the machines were frozen; some had fallen, and many had been stripped for parts. More ominously, a few of them sported hanged bodies, and one was adorned with a dangling cage containing a corpse. All the desiccated bodies wore weathered remains of white lab coats.

When they emerged onto the flatland of sagebrush and Joshua trees, they had to steer clear around the wooden ruins of a prison camp with skeletal guard towers and rusty razor wire.

Then there was the stout farm stronghold they passed several kilometers later. Its simple palisade and ditch spoke volumes. All these details fit with the Arc's projections of the slide into a dark age — a familiar pattern of superstition, then desperation, and finally the rut of repression.

They found Lone Pine transformed into a walled village beside Highway 395 running north and south. Albert was surprised that the villagers were not awestruck at the sight of a moving vehicle, nor were they fearful. To the contrary, around the stopped car gathered an openly curious crowd, providing a sea of hats, caps, and bonnets. They wore simple clothing, with most of the men in white shirts and gray pants, the women in dresses: this last a novelty for the Arc people.

Feeling self-conscious of his baby-blue coveralls, Albert stepped out to meet them. Before he could start his "we come in peace" speech, a man wearing a straw boater and a long black vest offered to sell him gasoline or diesel for the car, and quoted prices. This stunned Albert. The very definition of the "neobies" was that they should have no petroleum products, and their economic system was assumed to be the most primitive barter. Then he found that their units of economic exchange were small disks of silver and gold, giving Albert a much-needed boost of smug superiority. The Arcology used credits.

Albert aimed to awe the neobies by casually revealing Sivlo. He knew that when the superstitious are confronted by such "magic" there is a chance that they might become violent rather than worshipful, but he wanted to play this card upfront under conditions of his control. The time and mood seemed right, so he asked Maxine and Sivlo to bring out the trade goods.

The villagers surprised Albert again. They did not react to Sivlo, even when he spoke, and they seemed a bit disappointed in the steel hatchets, steel mirrors, flint and steel fire-making tools from the Arc. The crowd shrank as many drifted away.

Albert sold the trade goods for "coins," and then used many of them to buy cans of gasoline and diesel. The remaining coins and the fuel would be examined back at the Arc.

Having broken the social ice, Albert requested a meeting with the local headman. The merchant, perhaps delighted at his easy profit, personally took him to meet the mayor.

Albert saw his special talent of persuasion as being a lot like his hobby of lock-picking: where every personality was just a different type of lock, and there weren't really that many types. So when the mayor received Albert with open suspicion, it was almost too easy for Albert to use charm on him. While the mayor's statements were tight-lipped, still Albert extracted a wealth of information about the Owens Valley region of Inyo County.

When the team began their return to the Arcology, Albert mulled over what had happened. On the one hand the task was a bare-minimum success, but on the other hand Albert could not see an angle that they could use in drawing Lone Pine into the Arc's influence, making it an exasperating failure.

"The job is over," said Sivlo to Maxine. "Time to celebrate."

Maxine snorted and said, "Sure. Knock yourself out."

"Have I mentioned that I'm part Bonobo?"

"You're telling us all the time," said Albert.

"Maxine, among my people, we celebrate with whoo-pee."

"Huh," said Maxine, absently scratching her breast.

"So you and me, let's make whoopee."

"Huh?"

"Hey Sivlo, no," said Albert. "None of that."

"None? Not even a quickie? But I'm suffering!"

"None," said Albert. "And quit talking about it — you're making us males look bad." Carl nodded, sharing a look with him.

"Dirty monkey," said Maxine, giving a stone face frown.

Albert returned to the somber fact that the expedition had not gone very well. In the simulations, the people from the Arc first earned the trust of the neobies and then quickly became their technological priesthood. The "Atomic Power Priesthood" scenario was the favorite, often invoked as a shorthand term for the Mission Goal, whereas the less glamorous "Gasoline Refinery Priesthood" was known to be a more realistic scenario. But Lone Pine already had gasoline, produced at refineries far to the south, which meant that the most applicable scenario remaining was the "Agricultural Tech" one, among the least glamorous and lowest yielding racket of all.

The problem was that the post-collapse world was not nearly "collapsed" enough. But that was not the worst problem.

"The problem is that the Arc isn't hidden any more," said Albert. "We've broken cover. People know about us and will come looking. The clock is running and we don't have an angle yet."

"Turn it over to Weatherby," said Carl. "Just make the report and let the next team deal with it."

"We don't have that much time," said Albert, realizing that a return to the Arc without a formed plan would be a personal failure on his part.

As their armored car approached the farm stronghold again, Albert noticed a sombrero-wearing farmer there, leaning on his gatepost, watching them. Albert felt inspired, and told Carl to stop at the farm. Then, with his "we come in peace" lines ready, he stepped out to shape his destiny.

"Well hello, Albert!" said the farmer. "Can I help you with something?"

Albert was surprised again, but he recovered more quickly, asking, "You were in the crowd back there?"

"That's right, an' I's on my way home when you showed up. My name's Curtis."

Beneath his sombrero, the man's face was a weather-beaten red, as were his hands.

"Pleased to meet you, Curtis." Albert cast an appraising eye upon the silos, the farmhouse, and the barn, trying to remember that unit of "theoretical dirt-farming" he had struggled through years before. "This is a fine farm you've got."

"Thank you. It's a lot of work."

"Maybe I can help you to grow more crops with less work."

"That sounds mighty good. What's the secret?"

"The secret is that you only plant some of your fields, leaving the others to get back some of the nutrients that the growing plants used up."

"Sure, you mean crop rotation," said Curtis. "My fallow field's in the back this year."

"'Crop rotation,' that's it," said Albert, a weak smile trying to hide his disappointment. His one shot had come up short.

"Still," said Curtis, "I's always on the lookout for new secrets, even ones that some folk might call 'bad magic,' you know what I mean?"

"Yes," said Albert, his ears pricking up. "Yes, I do. What sort of secrets do you have in mind?"

The farmer looked from side to side, as if to assure himself they were not being overheard, and then said, "Petro-chem fertilizer."

"Powerful magic, indeed," said Albert. "You've used it before?"

Curtis nodded. "My pa had a sack hidden. I done used the last of it."

"Can you show me the sack?"

"I'll go get it."

After the farmer went away, Albert entered the car.

"I think we've got an angle here, " he said to Carl. "Can we make petrochemical fertilizer from our fuel reserves?"

"No." Carl rolled his eyes and pushed his glasses up. "That's from natural gas. The Haber Process, remember? First ammonia, then ammonia nitrate."

"So we would need an oil well."

"Right, and a refinery. The same as a gasoline priesthood."

"But you see what I mean?" asked Albert. "It would be like a cross between a gasoline god and a Squanto play, for a big agritech boost."

"I'm guessing you tried crop rotation? Look, if we don't have natural gas, then it is as far off as a decommissioned nuclear plant. It isn't going to happen. Hey, your farmer came back."

Albert went out. Curtis handed him an old blue plastic bag marked "Gaia Green." For an address it had "on Cottonwood by Owens Lake."

"Do you know where this place is?" asked Albert, indicating the sack.

"What place?" said Curtis, and Albert realized he was illiterate.

"How much do you need?"

"As much as I could get."

"How much would you pay for a full sack?"

They haggled for a few minutes.

"I think we can do business," said Albert. "Can I borrow this for a while? Thanks. I'll come back in a few days with an answer."

The team did a U-turn and drove back to the village, where they took Highway 395 south. After a few kilometers they came upon the semi-dustbowl of Owens Lake and took the Cottonwood off-ramp into a canyon to the west.

At the end of the canyon they found an industrial complex named "Gaia Green." A more recent graffiti depicted a green dragon head with jaws agape.

"Place looks like a refinery to me," said Albert.

"Yeah," said Carl, "but don't get your hopes up."

Leaving Sivlo to guard the car, the three humans gave the plant a quick tour. They found signs of periodic habitation, along with some minor vandalism. It was a showcase complex that had extracted natural gas from on-site shale deposits and processed it into fertilizer. Carl dryly stated the repairs necessary to make the complex operational. Albert became increasingly optimistic. Maxine was bored.

On the way back to the car, they came face to face with a gang of neo-barbarians. A group of men and several women, most wore ratty leather armor and carried rifles or shotguns. Each wore a different type of green hat.

"Who are you?" demanded their leader, a man singularly equipped with a flak jacket, a military officer's hat, and a large revolver.

"We come in peace," said Albert, raising his hands. "You must be the Heelas?"

"That's right," said the man, giving a little smile of satisfaction. "And this is Heela territory. So what are you giving us?"

Albert knew from talking with the mayor that the Heela gang had been chased into near exile by the Overlord of Inyo to the north. He pegged the gang leader as a man of penetrating insight, at the head of a group in sore need of an angle.

So Albert, playing it in the forthright manner, launched into his offer to pay the Heelas for providing security for the place, granting that the Heelas allowed the Arc people to restore the plant and get it running. He promised cash payment every two weeks, and asked if the Heelas would prefer that payment at a fixed rate or as a percentage of the profits. After some explanation on the percentage option, the leader Go-Jee chose the fixed rate. Albert closed the deal with a token advance from his cash on hand.

As the team drove away, Albert told the others, "See, by hiring them on, we get them on our side, and we begin their social rehabilitation. Win-win."

Carl said, "I don't know if you paid too much, or if you just bought Manhattan for some glass beads."

"It's better than that," said Albert. "This is going to work."

•

Albert had to convince the Arcology to go along with his plan, but unfortunately the leadership was largely immune to his powers of persuasion. First was Norman Weatherby, Director of Arc Administration, who seemed skeptical of the basic idea: "Shouldn't we first seek permission from the authority, this 'Overlord' of Inyo?"

"We aren't sure we can manufacture the stuff," said Albert. "If we can get the plant up and running, and if we can sell the product at a profit, then we will have more leverage." Weatherby winced at the term "profit," and he wiped his fingers on the sleeve of his white lab coat as if to clean them, but Albert continued. "Our buyers will be on our side. We will have a measure of income so we will know how much we can afford to pay in taxes, tribute, bribe, or kickback."

"'Bribe'? 'Kickback'?" sputtered Weatherby. "What's the — oh, never mind." He sighed with a slow shake of his head. "Now then, you have only the one potential buyer lined up, yes? Again, permissions come into play. You assume that you will be able to sell to all the farmers around Lone Pine, but what if they don't want it? What if the substance is forbidden by the mayor? Come back to me when you've investigated this further, in addition to getting the response from Tech Division."

Albert, with technical support from Carl, presented the case to Mr. Kim of the Technology Division. After hearing them out, Mr. Kim wanted to see the place himself. So the next morning the original team and three others crowded into the car, with the plan of dropping off some at Curtis's farm on the way to taking Mr. Kim and a couple of beefy guards over to the factory.

"I've been thinking about upgrading the security at Green Gaia," said Albert to Carl beside him. "The place seems so exposed. How about putting in a minefield?"

"We'd have to make some mines first."

"Right. At least a dozen or two, for starters. Could we make some?"

"Sure. A sensor module, a stick of dynamite with a blasting cap, and a battery pack should do it."

"Still, that's a lot of stuff for each one," said Albert, chewing his lip as the car slowed to stop at the farm. "A wall would probably be better . . ."

Albert, Maxine, and Sivlo got out of the car. Carl drove it away.

Upon meeting again with farmer Curtis, Albert first told him that the project was moving ahead, and then tried probing him about the attitude among farmers and villagers regarding petro-chem fertilizers.

Curtis was close-mouthed on the topic.

Albert turned on the charm, explaining that he was making Curtis his local expert, to deal with other farmers and the mayor. Seeing the farmer's face light up at that, Albert knew things were not too bad, and Curtis began talking.

"It's called 'bad magic,'" he said. "But nobody believes that stuff anymore. Most of the farmers, maybe all of them, will buy it, and the mayor is probably on our side."

"So there's no problem."

"Well," said Curtis, wringing his hands, "there are a few old timers in the village who would raise a fuss."

Albert nodded, glad to be getting a sense of a solution. "What can I do to help persuade them, or ease their minds?" he asked. "Is there some kind of gift that would make things right?"

"I believe a few cans of green paint would do it."

"'Green paint'?" It was so unexpected that Albert nearly laughed. "I'll see what I can do."

The meeting being concluded, the four of them walked to the village, where Curtis went alone to the mayor's place and the others went to the tavern, a building which Albert now noticed had green paint on the frames of the door and windows.

The trio whiled away the hours at the tavern. Albert bought drinks for villagers, gathered news and gossip, all the while avoiding comment on topics of a superstitious nature. When it was time for their return they went outside, meeting Curtis on his way in. The farmer seemed to suggest that his meeting with the mayor had gone well. Then the car arrived and the Arc people went home.

The next morning Albert made the case to Director Weatherby. After Albert was done, the Director nodded ponderously.

"Mr. Kim is onboard," he said. "That is an unexpected trophy for you. I'm still not sure about your hiring this neo-barbarian gang, but I appreciate how it relieves Sec Division from having to provide defense. On the other hand, this green paint scheme seems a bit uncertain — if it doesn't work out, that would be a real black eye."

"We'll cross that bridge, Director."

"Yes, yes we certainly will. For good, or for ill. But it occurs to me that we need an administrative balance to match the rank of Mr. Kim — as much as you might deserve the post, in light of all your effort in bringing it to fruition, still, you are only a supervisor."

Albert felt his stomach drop. A sudden numbness spread through his body.

"Perhaps you would like to take it yourself, Director?" he asked, his tongue thick.

"I'm flattered," said Weatherby. "You know, I envy you a bit — I hear the call to adventure, just like you do, but I simply cannot leave the Arc. My place is here. Which is why I've decided to give the post to Manager Zane Weatherby."

When Albert later complained about it to Carl, the engineer just grinned and said, "That's fair."

"What do you mean?"

"I don't get to be the chief engineer, and you don't get to be the administrator."

"Yeah, but at least Mr. Kim is a good engineer — Zane isn't a good administrator."

Carl winced and nodded.

"So that's where we are," he said. "I'm the driver and you're the paymaster for the Heelas."

"Which should be Maxine's job, I guess. But hey, back to the minefield idea — it would really be great if we could turn it on and off by remote signal, you know? Then we could plant bombs at the entrance point, at the gateway, rather than as a barrier."

"You know, the fertilizer has explosive properties, too . . ."

•

Busy weeks went by. Albert gave a few cans of green paint to Lone Pine. The engineers brought the factory online. The farmers around Lone Pine proved enthusiastic for the fertilizer, and each shipment was delivered in a natural gas powered truck. Carl began teaching Albert how to drive, and the pair also quietly experimented with making different explosive devices, only detonating them in the mountains near the Arcology.

The Overlord of Inyo made a surprise appearance with four battlewagons on a day when a load of fertilizer was ready for shipment to Lone Pine. Conveniently for the Overlord, it was a time when Carl and the armored car were away at the Arcology.

Zane Weatherby ordered all personnel to assemble in the parking lot to face this challenge — the twenty Arc people fronted by the nine Heelas with their weapons at the ready. For a moment Albert wondered what Zane would do, now that he actually had to do something, but then Zane told him to go parley with the visitors.

Happy at the opportunity, Albert went over to negotiate.

There were four principals and six subordinates that Albert took to be bodyguards. The four wore metal helmets and what looked like chainmail armor. Their underlings had reinforced leather armor.

A bodyguard stopped Albert within a few meters of the group and looked him over for pistol or knife. Finding none, he nodded to the visiting group, then asked, "Your name?"

"Albert."

"Albert, these here are the lords of Inyo — that's Lord of Bishop, Lord of West Bishop, Lord of Dixon/Meadow, Lord of Lone Pine, and Lord of Independence, who's the Overlord of Inyo. My lords, this is Albert."

"'Lord of Lone Pine'?" said Albert in confusion. "I wasn't aware Lone Pine had a lord."

"He's new," said the Overlord. "Brand new. My son starts today, after we finish here."

"Ah, I see," said Albert, a burning sensation in his gut. "Congratulations on your elevation."

Albert read the Overlord as a tough lock to pick. Charming wouldn't work, so he went with being forthright.

Albert began his offer, aiming for either a one-time "elevation tribute" to mark the occasion of the new Lord of Lone Pine, or an ongoing deep discount price for the "government."

Unfortunately the Overlord was uninterested.

"The time for such petty bribery is past," he said. "This business is unregulated, unlicensed, and unlawful. That is why, for the protection of the people, I am taking it over. Heelas, disarm the slaves!"

The Heelas immediately turned their guns upon the Arc people.

"Mr. Overlord," said Albert, shaken by the sudden turn of events, "with all due respect, I think that you would get more work out of free men than slaves."

"We will find out."

"But if you kill the technicians, who will work the machinery?"

"I doubt it will come to that. Besides, you're all white coats, and you know what we do to white coats."

"Sir, we are technicians, not white coats."

"Slavery is better than death," said the Overlord. "Now give me the keys to the delivery truck."

"Please, sir, don't take our truck. Allow us to load the fertilizer into your vehicles."

"No. Give me the keys — I won't ask again."

Albert gave him the keys.

"Good," said the Overlord. "Now go sit down on the ground with your friends, under the watchful eyes of your new masters."

Stunned and numb, Albert turned and started walking to the prisoners. The Heela leader Go-Jee passed him, grinning broadly. The other Heelas were giddy with their new status, and many drifted toward the Overlord and his retinue.

Albert dropped down heavily next to Maxine at the edge of the clump.

"This is not acceptable," said Zane from the center of the group.

"I'm very disappointed, myself," said Albert. "I had a deal with Go-Jee. I always paid on time, and he turns like this."

Albert's worldview was turned upside down, and he struggled to get a grip on it. He had a deal with the Heelas, but then the Heelas apparently had used that to get back in good graces with the Overlord. Albert had not been given a chance to make a counter offer. He felt stupid, naïve, and overly trusting.

And now this! The Overlord was no more than a bandit, performing the ambush robbery they were always a-fraid of during a delivery run. Well, it was worse than that, since he was also enslaving the Arc people. Albert felt responsible and his blood began to boil with anger.

It was painful to watch the victors backslapping each other and whooping it up. The Overlord climbed into the truck bed to sit atop the mound of bags. His men roared with approval.

Albert glanced at the guards around them, a man and three women. All eyes were on the Overlord. Albert leaned to Maxine and murmured, "Get ready."

She looked incredulous, but nodded slightly.

The vehicles started up and moved into a formation with two battlewagons in front of the treasure truck and two behind. Half of the Heelas were cheering and running alongside the truck, giving the Overlord a send off.

Albert pulled the gadget from his pocket. The nearest guard turned and said, "Hey!" Albert opened the panel and pushed the button.

There was a deafening explosion in the center of the motorcade. The Overlord went up in two pieces.

Maxine sprang up and decked the nearest guard. Albert tackled the next one, but the man broke free and blasted him in the leg with his shotgun. Writhing in pain on the ground, Albert saw the guard work the pump in slow motion, saw the big shotgun barrel moving toward his head, when shots from Maxine sent the guard to the ground. Albert fell over then, and through tunnel vision saw a female guard shoot Maxine, who promptly gunned her down. Maxine was shooting at someone else when the picture winked out.

Someone was poking him and it hurt like fire. Albert suddenly sat up.

"Hey, easy, easy," said Sivlo the medic, ministering to Albert's wound. "You're all right."

"Is it bad?"

"Not so bad."

"How long was I out?" asked Albert.

"Just a few minutes."

"What happened?" demanded Zane Weatherby, leaning in. "What did you do?"

"I cut off the head," said Albert with defiance. "Now grab a gun and come on. Sivlo, check Maxine, I think she's wounded."

"Hey!" shouted Maxine, over at the blast site. "We got survivors."

Sivlo looked at Albert for leadership. Albert turned to Zane, who said, "Well, ah — "

"We cannot have prisoners," said Albert through gritted teeth. "Kill them all!" he shouted.

Zane nodded in resignation.

The Arc people shied away from this, so Albert did it himself, executing lords, bodyguards, and Heelas. Then Albert had the others strip the corpses of weapons and armor.

Albert was crouched down, looking over this equipment, when Mr. Kim returned.

"Good to see you up and around," said Mr. Kim. "I called the Arc on the radio, told them about this."

"Was that Zane's idea?"

"Not really." He studied the gear for a moment before saying, "This is bad. The start of a lot of fighting."

"Better than being slaves," said Albert, fingering the rings on a bloodied chainmail shirt.

"Yes! I'm not criticizing what you did — in fact, I'm very lucky that you did it — it's just not what we had originally envisioned."

"I know what you mean," said Albert, standing up and turning to face him. "We tried so hard to be non-threatening, but then that set us up, you know? By looking weak, we invited attack and enslavement."

"You're right," said Mr. Kim. "But now, with some field adjustments, the Mission really begins!"

KARMA HUNTER

The wind-up alarm clock rang, waking Vince Forcetti to another day of mutant hunting in San Francisco.

Using hot water from a thermos flask, he washed his face and shaved around his pencil-thin mustache. After breakfast he took a cup of instant coffee into the living room and fired up the short wave radio.

"Outpost Karma calling East Pac Two," he said into the mike. "Outpost Karma calling East Pac Two. Come in, over."

"This is East Pacific Two," said the radio. "We read you, Outpost Karma. Please stand by for situation update, over." Vince sipped his coffee for half a minute before the other continued. "Here is your twelve-hour report for August 29. Clear weather continues to hold, despite the season. Satellite recon shows access points one and two remain clear. Heavy traffic in sector Indigo One, repeat, Indigo One. Probable cluster forming. Please investigate. Continuing traffic at hot spot in sector Charlie Four, repeat, Charlie Four. Please investigate, over."

Vince nodded to himself. The two bridges into San Francisco, cut after the evacuation in order to keep mutants from walking across from the north or the east, were clear. A group of mutants numbering ten or more had come together in the Castro District, and a new group had apparently infiltrated the cordon sanitaire to take up residence over by the Broadway Tunnel, a place he had cleared out a few weeks earlier.

Vince repeated the work order back and tried to sign off, but the other guy reminded him to give his Public Service Announcement. Vince hesitated, feeling it pointless or even degrading so many months after the trickle of survivors had dried up, but finally he did it, rattling off the invitation of a lifeline.

"This is Karma Hunter with a message for any survivors within the sound of my voice — California, Oregon, and Nevada," he said. "I can offer you food, shelter, and transportation to a safe place. Meet me at Coit Tower in San Francisco, between noon and three. It looks like a fire hose nozzle, on top of a hill. You can't miss it."

"Outpost Karma, over and out."

•

The plague had come from a comet. Astronomers had known that these icy bodies held the building blocks of life, and even theorized that comets had seeded the primordial Earth with life itself. But it seemed that there were competing life-types, and the plague from space was proving to be an evolutionary challenge for humanity.

The DNA-altering disease swept the continents. Naturally immune creatures, animal and human, amounted to only seven per cent of their respective populations. The uninfected people fled to islands since the mutants could not cross water, lacking the wit and the motor skills to operate vehicles.

Vince drove his pickup truck around in the Castro, looking for signs of the proto cluster spotted from orbit. It turned out to be fairly obvious — a large number of freshly gnawed human bones lying in the gore-splattered street outside an apartment building. The cluster had fed well upon a few smaller groups of weaker mutants, the strong preying upon the weak in a dog-eat-dog world.

Vince shook his head as he got out of the truck. *If they had the intelligence to hide the bodies, they could go further. But then my job would be harder.*

He counted the dead and estimated that the victorious cluster had ten or twelve members. He checked his submachine gun, then took up his tool bag and entered the building. He didn't bother with the basement, since mutants paradoxically behaved as though they were still human, and cluster mutants even more so, tending to live upstairs whenever possible.

He found an engorged female sleeping on a daybed on the second floor. It woke up and hissed at him, the typical response of a Class 1 mutant. He used a mallet-driven stake on the "ghoul" to avoid disturbing the others. It was just an underling — the real prize would be the leader.

Vince found the Class 2 mutant on the third floor. It was far more human-seeming than a ghoul. It spoke, pleading at first, and then it fought. Vince used the Mac-10 to tear open its chest. The rest of the nest roused for that, and Vince had some hot fighting before they were all dead.

Then he loaded the bodies into the truck and drove over to the pit to burn them. Theory held the Class 2 strain as a more virulent form of the plague, possibly carried by the cluster members as well as the leader. According to this, timely burning was essential to ensure that the strain would not spread. There was also the more prosaic reason that burning corpses removed them as a mutant food source.

By the time he finished that job it was nearly noon. Vince drove over to Coit Tower and ate his lunch, looking out over the silent city. There was nobody around the distinctive structure. Nobody living, at least — just scattered piles of bone and hanks of hair. The main task of the hunters was to get the Class 2s, to clear them off the peninsula in preparation for re-colonization. The rest of the mutants would be wiped out through attrition, like a wildfire that burns out for lack of fuel.

Vince drove over to a house near Broadway Tunnel and cleared out a group of ghouls. After he hauled them to the pit and burned them, it was getting close to three o'clock. He went back to Coit Tower and waited, sitting by the eucalyptus trees.

She came walking up the grassy road in broad daylight — a survivor!

"Hey!" Vince shouted to her, waving.

She hesitated, then turned and started running.

"Wait!" he yelled, following her. "I'm not going to hurt you!"

She didn't dare dash for the steep stairway on the left, she could only hope to outrun him on the road, but she slowed down as if realizing her mistake. He caught up with her when she stopped.

"Why did you run?" he asked, panting.

"You were in the shade," she gasped. "I was scared." She flared into anger. "I mean, look at you! Splattered with blood, and soot!"

Vince's eyes went wide at her scolding, but then he burst out laughing. "I'm sorry," he said. "You're right, I *am* a mess. I'm sure I smell like a monster, too!" He started to put out his hand, but then held it back against his chest. "I'm Vince, the local hunter."

"I'm Ruth." She offered her hand, and after a pause he shook hands with her. Her hand was warm, not like the flesh of the mutants, whose body temperature was twenty degrees lower, making them seem dead.

"Come on, I'll take you back to the outpost."

They started walking back up Telegraph Hill to his truck.

"You couldn't be from around here?" he said.

"No, I'm from out by Sacramento," she said. "A kind of fortress community, a few families behind a strong wall.

My husband —" She shook her head, fighting off the grief that flashed across her face. "My husband died, after lasting so long."

"I'm sorry."

"Thank you." She looked away, towards the Transamerica Tower that rose like a stretched pyramid from the Financial District. "When he was gone, there was nothing for me there anymore. So I drove my car down here to the Bay. It was a nasty surprise finding the bridge cut!"

"I can imagine."

"You should mention that in your announcement."

"Maybe so."

"Well, anyway, I drove south through San Jose, then north, up through Silicon Valley until South San Francisco, where the gas ran out."

"Where did you leave the car?"

"I couldn't even tell you."

"You came up the 101, right?"

"Yeah, but I got off somewhere to scrounge for gas."

"Maybe I'll find it later. What color is it?"

"It's a green Prius."

"Great, thanks," said Vince. "Now, your husband died . . . of plague?"

"Yes."

"How long ago?"

"About two weeks ago. Ten days. So if I caught it, it should have shown up after a week, right?"

"Yeah. But maybe you're immune."

"That would be a relief."

"But then you'd have to become a hunter, or a scavenger."

"That hardly seems fair!"

"It's a world-wide forest fire," he said. "Everyone has to pitch in."

"True."

Vince drove them to the outpost, a two-story single-family house at the southern end of the city. He got on the radio and called in her helicopter ride for the next day, then made dinner for two. She began eating with gusto, but before long she was only picking at the food.

"You were married?" she asked.

"Yes."

"Children?"

"Yes," he said, falling into the familiar conversation when meeting survivors. "They all died, wife and daughters. The girls didn't inherit my immunity. Maybe it is recessive."

"I'm so sorry."

"Thank you. But cheer up! Tomorrow you will be flying out to Avalon."

"Avalon?"

"The main city on Catalina Island."

"Is that — is that where everybody is?"

"No, it is just the first stage — a purgatory place between hell and human. Vancouver Island is the other one for the West Coast."

She excused herself to use the bathroom. He heard her vomiting.

"Let me tell you something about Avalon," he said when she came back to the table. "A lot of people there suffer from guilt, survivor guilt. They struggled, they fought, and they were lucky enough to get to the island, but then once they get there, they start to feel bad. Unworthy. Unclean."

"Do you have those feelings?"

"Not so much," he said. "I keep working out here — maybe that's the cure!" She gave a wan smile. "Well anyway, you will be in quarantine at Avalon for a week. Then you will be released to the city — and with fifteen thousand people, it is like a real city! No more running and hiding, no more scrounging and scavenging. After quarantine you can look into your options for relocating."

As he was talking, the mutants had come forth in the darkness to begin their subhuman fight for survival.

A pack of five came to the door, drawn by the scent of humans, but then repulsed by the garlic garland armoring the door. Moaning and grunting, they battered at the boarded up windows, trying to break in. Their noise drew a second pack and the two groups fought, the victors feeding on the tainted flesh of the losers.

"God, it's so horrible," said Ruth.

"Yes, but you are safe now. Tomorrow you will be far away."

Vince and Ruth retired to separate bedrooms to catch what sleep they could.

In the morning, Vince called her to breakfast. Ruth looked pale and drawn, as though she hadn't slept all night. After a light meal, she ran to the bathroom. Her sounds of agony prompted Vince to try and help her. He burst in to find her injecting herself with a syringe.

"What's this?" he said.

"It's nothing," she said, already looking much better. She grabbed up an open packet of preloaded syringes.

Suddenly her inability to keep food down took on a sinister cast, as did her haggard look before the injection.

"You have the plague," he said, dumbfounded.

She whipped out a small automatic pistol and shot him in the chest. He crumpled to the floor, darkness washing over him.

He was dimly aware of things being moved around, as if his replacement had arrived for his stint weeks ahead of schedule and was checking the supplies and equipment. The sound of the truck starting up brought him to full consciousness. He tried to rise, only to hear it drive away.

Vince struggled up, clutching at his bloody side, and staggered to the supply closet. He had to make the emergency call, but he found that the satellite phone was gone, along with the back-up radio. He stumbled over to the living room to confirm that the radio was missing from there, too. Ruth had been thorough.

Vince used the medical kit to patch himself as best he

could before he bled out.

A green car pulled up in eerie silence. Vince grabbed his Mac-10 and went out the backdoor to hide in the bushes of the backyard jungle. He heard mutants enter the house and search, making out the voices of three men. After a while he saw the house was on fire. He stifled a moan, forced himself to stay still when his body screamed for him to fight or flee. The car drove off.

Frightened, Vince was wounded and on his own, no longer safe in the daytime. Shelter, food, and water were now at the top of his list. He had to warn the world about this terrible new menace of daytime mutants. Although he had no radio, he knew Avalon would send a helicopter when he failed to report later, so he started limping toward the airport, six miles away across uncleared mutant territory.

Before sunset came he holed up in an upper floor room at the Comfort Inn, across the 101 from the airport. Through the night he heard the mutants down on the street, but luckily they left him alone.

In the morning he made his slow way over to the airport, where he followed the truck's trail in the road grass, the track made by Karma Hunters driving back and forth from SFO. When new tracks left the old trail he gave a soft laugh seeing where they went — it was the long term parking structure. Ruth was behaving as though the world hadn't ended, probably relying on the memories of when she was human. At least she had the sense to park the truck on the ground floor, which is where he found it.

"All right!" he said, grinning from ear to ear as he hobbled over to it. He had never been so happy to see the trusty pickup truck, with its roll bar floodlights and its solid tires. He found the key still in the ignition, and the engine started right up.

Buoyed by this good fortune, he eagerly searched the cab and bed for the short wave radios and the satellite phone, but she had gotten rid of them somewhere. The truck's dashboard radio could pick up short wave, but it couldn't broadcast.

He turned on the radio and drove out of the structure, over to the airfield where he found a hidden spot from which he could watch the helicopter landing area. Immediately he saw something unusual out there on the tarmac, something close to the ground. Vince got the monocular from the glove compartment, and through it he spied a neat stack of boxes.

Supplies. As usual, the pilot had taken the opportunity to bring along cargo, and then he had left it there before taking up the passenger.

But now it sat there like the cheese-bait in a mousetrap. The day mutants might be watching it. If he went to get it, he would lose his advantage. The main thing was the helicopter.

Having heard nothing on the radio, he turned it off.

As the hours went by, his feeling of success grudgingly gave way to a growing unease. He wondered where the helicopter could be, since its hours of operation were limited. When he had failed to make radio check in, that should have sent them out in some force in the morning, and yet it was past noon.

With the hope of a helicopter rescue that day fading, the importance of the supplies out there in the open grew larger. In the end he drove out, grabbed the stuff, and drove back to the hotel.

Sunset found him glued to the truck radio, hoping to hear something. When the familiar voice came on asking for Outpost Karma to respond, he felt relief, since he had been fighting off worry that things had gone horribly wrong at Avalon — that Ruth had somehow destroyed the place already. Still, he was puzzled that the caller was not giving any explanation as to why the helicopter hadn't come.

The caller repeated himself. After the third repetition, Vince was about to turn it off when he suddenly heard the answer, "Outpost Karma here, over."

For an instant Vince wondered if he had spoken out loud.

"Good to hear you back on the air, Karma," said the guy in Avalon. "Have you found a new place yet? Over."

"No new place yet," said the imitation Vince. "I'm still salvaging stuff from the fire and staying at a temporary place. Over."

"Roger that, Karma. We will let the work orders stack up until after you are re-established. Over."

"Okay. That makes sense. Over."

"Just make sure to check in at the usual times. Over."

"Will do. Thanks. Over and out."

"East Pacific Three, over and out."

Vince sat there, stunned. He shook himself, turned off the radio, and hurried up to his hideout, his mind reeling with the new reality he had stumbled into.

A mutant was imitating his voice on the radio. There would be no helicopter rescue.

"How long can they keep that up?" he asked himself. He decided they were buying time, maybe a few weeks. Which seemed too short a time to achieve anything, until he remembered that Ruth's quarantine would be over in less than a week.

Could he track them down and get a radio or the phone back? He might be able to track them if they were driving the hybrid car at speed around the area every day, since he could hear a gas-burning engine for miles in a dead city, but if they remained close to their base, or holed up completely, then it was a slim chance.

Could he do some sort of triangulation thing when they were broadcasting? No. Besides, he was wounded and there were at least three of them, and they might have a number of lower mutants as well.

The goal is not revenge, he reminded himself. *The goal is to get the news to Avalon as soon as possible. Catching Ruth before she leaves quarantine in five days.*

He considered driving to L.A. In the pre-plague world such a thing could be done in nine hours. Just a trip to Disneyland —

The memory hit at all of his senses. The steering wheel's soft plastic in his hands, the long straight road of the 5 ahead, the delicate scent of his wife's perfume mixed with the aromas of almond blossoms and hay from outside. His wife beside him, and the girls in the back counting cows and horses. He felt the razor-burn on his cheek from early-morning shaving. But mostly that happy anticipation of being on the road to Disneyland.

All of which made him wince with sharp grief. That was the plan, to make it to Avalon in one or two days.

It took him a day to scrounge up supplies for the trip — food, water, and gasoline — and then he made the ten-hour drive to Los Angeles, where he met up with the scavenging crews from Santa Catalina Island.

•

"How bad is it, Forcetti?" asked Chief Bryant the moment Vince walked into his office.

"Not so bad," said Vince. "I'm lucky, the bullet ricocheted off my rib."

"You should be on bed rest."

"No way. I've got to question Ruth."

"About that — "

"Don't tell me she got out!"

"No, no, we've got her," said Bryant, grunting a laugh. "But look, this whole thing is pretty elaborate, don't you think?"

"Well, yeah. The fact that they've got a guy impersonating me on the radio shows a lot of organization."

"That's right," said Bryant. "We've been infiltrated by something new. Call it a Class 3, with a sophisticated group behind it."

"God, she could infect so many around here," said

Vince.

"I don't think she will," said Bryant. "I think she's a scout, or she's trying to get to a haven island before she does anything like that. But you're the one who met her — you should tell me everything."

Vince gave his report. After asking a few questions, Bryant drummed his fingers on the desk.

"She only had eight or nine of those syringes?" he said. "Sounds like she's going to do something fast."

"Or she knows how to make the stuff," said Vince. "She only needs a one-week supply to get through quarantine."

"This is how we're going to do it. We release her — "

"You're kidding me!"

"No, listen. We release her on schedule and she leads us to her friends."

"But we could beat it out of her *now*."

"It's bigger than her."

"She could infect others."

"We've got some bad apples here, and I have to find them."

Vince glared at him for a few tense moments, then gave in. "Oh, all right."

"Good. You are undercover now. Shave off your mustache and dye your hair in the john right there. Here are some new clothes and a key to a room at the Excelsior. You've got to follow her, but not too close."

"Is that shaving and dying necessary?" asked Vince. "People who've known me for years will still recognize me, and say I've got a new look."

"Yes, it is necessary. 'Vince' is working outpost Karma — and you are his cousin Frankie, come to visit from Hawaii. So that's what people will say, that you look like your cousin. But listen, you have to avoid all the people who really know you, *capiche?*"

"Yeah, yeah. You don't have to use the lingo on me."

"All right then. Get to it." Still Vince was hesitating.

"What is it now?"

"I've never dyed before," said Vince. "Could you, uh, help me?"

•

Vince began shadowing Ruth on the day she was released. The mutant's activities seemed 'human' enough, except she skipped lunch. Vince grabbed a bison burger to go.

Before the plague, Avalon had been a resort town with a fluctuating population of around 5,000. Now the permanent population was three times that, making for crowded quarters with suburbs of tent cities and shanty-towns. As darkness fell, Vince followed Ruth through one of the rougher neighborhoods. She found a cat and picked it up, petting it as she walked into a large dark building.

Vince followed, arriving at the lobby just in time to see the basement door close. After waiting a few moments, he opened the door softly to peek inside. The basement light was on, showing a stairway going down to a place filled with a lot of dusty junk. But there was no sign of Ruth, and Vince thought she had somehow given him the slip. Then he heard the muffled scream of a cat, cut off suddenly, as if a closing door had stopped the sound.

Vince went down the stairs. Finding a door, he listened at it. Hearing nothing, he opened it to discover an empty utility closet about ten feet deep. Again, the light was on in a room that had no people. He went in, closing the door, his senses stretching out for any clues. There was an earthy smell, no doubt from the garden supply sacks in the scatter of litter on the floor, alongside empty plastic drink bags of cherry punch, that made the place seem like a potting shed used by teens as a club house. An odd place for a break room, but maybe that's all it was.

Vince picked up one of the drink bags and was startled to discover it was a blood bag, a medical item. He grabbed a garden supply bag and found it was bloodmeal.

There was a weird, muffled sound coming through the walls. The sound was coming from the back wall, and with his ear pressed against it he could make out what sounded like a mutant pack attack, the cries of several ghouls feeding.

He left quickly and took up a surveillance spot where he could watch the building. Ruth came out an hour later, without the cat. He waited five minutes and then went back to the utility closet. With determined searching he found how to open the secret door.

The room beyond was another basement, this time lit by lights as bright as daylight. From the top of the stairs he could see bones and debris from many a mutant feast scattered on the open floor, and three closed doors. Vince drew his pistol and went down the stairs. Listening at each of the doors, he heard a faint snoring behind one. He nodded to himself, but still he had to fight down his hunter impulse to kill them all while they were torpid. Instead he left the building to retrieve a fingerprint kit.

•

"That was quick thinking, taking their prints," said Bryant as they waited for his computer to match the prints. "And it takes a lot of nerve to pull it off. They give you any trouble?"

"No," said Vince, yawning. Dawn was streaming into the hotel room they used for meetings. "They were all gorged on feeding. Still, it was pretty creepy."

"A ghoul farm," said Bryant with a grim laugh. He shook his head. "She feeds them scraps and then feeds off of them. It must be a lot of work, keeping them supplied."

"There must be more than one mutant involved," said Vince. "She didn't do all this by herself."

"So there must be a bunch of these Class-3s already here to have all this in place," said Bryant. "She's not the first, she's only the most recent."

"She can drive, since she took my truck," said Vince. "She can use a gun, and a hypo. How can we tell a Class 3 from a human?"

"Keep 'em in lock up overnight," said Bryant, "and see what you have in the morning."

"A blood test would probably show it."

"They're not going to sit still for that!"

Two of the fingerprints came back as belonging to missing persons, people who had disappeared months before. Guilt-ridden survivors went missing often enough to be a solid statistic, and sometimes they came back. The numbers hadn't changed recently, but maybe it was just too soon to tell.

The third mutant was identified as a survivor who had developed the plague while in quarantine, subsequently euthanized and cremated at the Catalina pit.

"Well," said Bryant, his mouth a tight line. "Looks like it's an inside job. She has a friend or friends over at Quarantine."

"How many people are involved in a kill and burn over there?"

"Supposed to be two or three, but you know, one can do it. Looks like our person of interest is Leon Pierre."

"He's been here for months," said Vince, scanning the information on the screen.

"Yeah, came in from Vancouver, which is where he was processed."

•

The case was like a ticking time bomb — the hunt was on. Bryant brought a few detectives into the investigation, starting with a day in secret quarantine to establish they weren't day-mutant infiltrators. Vince felt the burning drive to discover the conspiracy.

On Monday Ruth booked passage on a ship bound for

Hawaii, a three-week voyage. That night Vince had a dream of confronting Ruth in an interrogation room. After a moment of surprise at seeing him alive, she downplayed her attempted murder, saying, "I would've stayed and made sure you were dead. It shows a mercy on my part, a trait that has proven my undoing."

"I think you were in a hurry," said Vince. "You had a helicopter to catch. Besides, there was a cleanup squad coming to tie up any loose ends."

She looked away, saying nothing . . .

On Tuesday Vince found three more ghoul farms through surveillance and investigating patterns of unusual electricity usage. Since each farm could support one mutant, this suggested the presence of perhaps two more mutants in addition to Ruth and Leon. In his recurring dream, he said, "I hope you are comfortable here? The blood and the serum are adequate?"

"Yes," she said. "I — yes."

"Good. We're not sure about your mutant biology, but we are learning very quickly. For example, your good friend Leon started to fall apart without the serum, as if he were degenerating into a ghoul."

"That's a lie."

Vince smiled blandly, shrugged . . .

On Wednesday Leon booked passage on the same ship as Ruth, the tenth and final passenger. Back in the dream that night, Vince said, "As you can guess, this whole thing has really shaken up our worldview. We naively thought that time was on our side, but now it seems clear that time allowed you aristocrat mutants to rise up. An agricultural civilization based upon human cattle."

"As if you consider ghouls to be *human* . . ."

On Thursday Vince located the serum lab supplying the mutants with their daily doses, a place being run by a few twisted immunes. Again in his dreams, Vince questioned the monster: "So you have these plantations, these death camps. You have organized yourselves into whole towns, perhaps even small cities."

"Leon told you this, so why bother with me? I know nothing. I'm the weakest link."

"But why would you, your people, try to infiltrate us if time was on your side? You could continue to develop in secret, consolidating all the resources of the ruined world. We must have something that you want, something you need. What is it?"

"I don't know such things, I am only a soldier following orders . . ."

On Friday night, Vince wasn't sleeping, he was part of the raid to get Ruth. Other teams were moving in on the serum lab and the dwellings of all the other nine passengers.

As they entered the apartment building, Vince felt his hunter instincts come on, which was strange in a place illuminated with hall lights. There were no cluster ghouls to deal with here, just the one monster up on the fourth floor. They went up the stairs quickly yet quietly, and found the door to her room.

They smashed the door open and rushed in, Vince at the front. Their flashlight beams caught Ruth standing in her nightgown in the middle of the room, as if she had sensed them coming some time ago.

She was clutching at a whistle she wore on a chain around her neck.

Someone turned on the light as Vince continued forward to grab her. Like a panther, she twisted and leaped to the balcony's sliding glass door. She jerked it open and started through, the whistle now in her mouth.

Vince grabbed her wrist, halting her flight.

"*You*," she said, the whistle falling from her lips. She smiled and relaxed as if giving up, then jabbed him in the eye, twisting out of his grip in the instant of his surprise. Then she launched herself off the balcony.

For a moment Vince thought she had actually flown away. Then he heard the sound of her body hitting the pavement below.

When he got back down to the street he saw that Bryant had put handcuffs on her wrists and ankles. His hopes were dashed when Bryant saw him and shook his head.

"She's dead," he said. "But I'm not taking any chances."

"Damn," said Vince. "I hope they have better luck with Leon."

"What's with the whistle?"

"I don't know. I didn't hear anything."

"Maybe it's ultrasonic, or something."

"None of the others are that close around here."

"That we know of."

Vince squatted down and picked up the whistle. Turning it, he saw the mouthpiece was crumpled, with a few drops of honey-like fluid there.

Vince dropped it as if it were too hot to hold.

"What?" said Bryant.

"Some fluid in there."

"Spit," said Bryant. "Or blood."

"No, I don't think so. Maybe poison."

"Poison? Huh. Yeah, could be."

"Like a spy with a suicide pill," said Vince, standing up. "So we couldn't question her."

"You know, maybe this is a silver lining," said Bryant. "Or could be even better than that, like pure gold."

"What do you mean? She won."

"If it turns out she poisoned herself, now we will know what poison works on them. A weapon. Maybe it isn't even toxic to humans."

"Wow." Vince looked down at the corpse. "But everything is changed now. It isn't a 'forest fire' anymore, it really is a war — a war of extinction."

THE WALKING, WEEPING
PROTOTYPES

When Noah walked into the mobile command post, the frazzled commander took one look at him and said, "A robot. I have my hands full with one already, and headquarters sends me another one."

"I am the same type as Victor," said the civilian, a humanoid robot standing 175 cm tall. His human clothes softened his appearance overall, but his exposed head, hands, and feet were clearly metal. "I may be able to reason with him. I'm Noah."

"I know — the Warlord's Office told me that much," said the commander with a grimace. "Forget what I said. Haven't slept. I'm Makali." He nodded a seated bow, but kept his eyes on Noah. "Tell me your type."

"We are prototypes for the Seeders," said Noah. "Of course, there are no Seeders on Earth."

"Huh," said Makali, rubbing his stubbly chin. "That must be very rare. I would've guessed 'butler' or 'valet,' something like that. How many of you are there?"

"A few dozen. We are loners by design."

"Well, Victor's acting like some kind of warbot — not

116

that I've ever seen one — who has? But his crazy demands are more like what a Seeder would give, I guess."

"Demands?"

"First he asked for a starship." Makali paused for a sip of coffee. "We reminded him that there were only three, and they left just before the Great War. Then we had to convince him that those trips are strictly one-way — they're never coming back. So now he wants a desert island somewhere, a place he can raise all the orphans he's holding hostage."

"How many kids?"

"Around thirty, all little ones — the big ones got away — but he seems to be killing them. And that seems more like what a warbot would do."

"Does he really have a bomb, or is he bluffing?"

"He gave us a convincing serial number for a one kiloton nuke," said Makali. "We've evacuated the city. You look fairly human — have you got any special powers I should know about? Does he?"

"No, we are close to human. We even eat human food."

"Really?" said Makali with surprise. "I've never heard of that one. Can I get you something to eat?"

"No, thank you."

"Well then, what happened to make a civybot turn into . . . this?"

"Please tell me how it started."

"The orphanage is about one and a half kilometers in from here," said Makali. "It's an old building — glass in front, bunkers inside. So at eighteen hundred yesterday the dining hall was full and a car crashed through the front door. Two or three humans were in the car, with the robot and the bomb. The humans all ran away, leaving Victor holed up in the dining hall. There's only the one way into that room. There are high windows to let light in."

"It is a stand off."

"Yes, for eight or nine hours now. Seems like a suicide

mission to send anyone in. That bomb goes off, it'll kill everyone within a kilometer." He paused for another sip. "I can only see a few ways for this to play out. If we rush him, it's all or nothing. If we wait, he kills more kids, but maybe not all of them. If we agree to his demands, maybe we can pick him off at some point before he gets to the plane."

Makali drained the cup. "Well, that's all I've got. What are you going to do?"

"With your permission I'm going to walk in there and talk him out of it." Noah produced a card from his trench coat pocket. "I need a waiver on the Fifty Meter Limit, in writing."

"'Fifty Meter Limit'?"

"Yes, we are forbidden to be within fifty meters of elementary schools, children's hospitals, and the like. This was a condition of our getting citizenship."

"Did Victor go berserk just because he went inside the limit?"

"Absolutely not," said Noah. "It is more than that. After all, he's got a bomb — that's premeditated. I suspect the humans, since Seeders have no use for bombs."

"Tell me something," said Makali. "Did you fight in the Great War?"

"No. We were built for science, for colonization, not for warfare."

Makali took the card, ran it through the reader on his slate, then signed it with a pen.

"Thank you," said Noah as he took the card back.

"Yeah," said Makali. "Say, you got a gun?"

"No."

"Want one?"

"No, thank you."

"All right, it's your funeral," said Makali. "But listen, even if you can't talk him down, you can find out important details for us. Like, does he have a dead man switch for the bomb, or is it a button he has to push?"

•

It was four in the morning when Noah left the mobile command post. As he walked down the street of the emptied city, a dry south wind, the Santa Ana, brought him the scent of eucalyptus as it rustled the bamboo groves — it was fire season in *Kalifernya*. He tried to remember the old towns of the area, recalling only that the first atomic bomb had been invented nearby.

He arrived at the orphanage. The entry room was trashed, nearly filled by the wrecked car. The sound of broken glass being crushed beneath his feet reminded Noah to adjust his audio input levels. He set filters to exclude everything below and above sound at around the level of normal conversation. When the first whiff of blood came he felt a churning inside, so he turned off his olfactory sense, thinking, *Hear no evil, smell no evil.*

"Victor, I'm coming to talk to you," he said. "It is Noah, your little brother."

He broadcast a simple IFF identity beacon a few times before he heard a response over the internal radio. An IFF query from VCT-15 came, and his reply verified that he was NO-A.

"Noah!" Victor's hearty voice boomed down the corridor. "Come on in. End of the hallway."

Noah went down the corridor and entered the dining hall. The tables were scattered against the walls, leaving open space in the middle of the room. The twenty-three children, ranging in age from one to four, were huddled in the back corner on the left. Just glancing at them gave Noah another churning feeling. Being at the edge of a vortex.

He focused on Victor and the suitcase nuke at the center of the room, the robot a gleaming metal humanoid free of human clothing.

"Close the door behind you," said Victor, raising his fist to show the detonator he held, and how it was linked by cable to the bomb. "Did you come alone?"

"Yes," said Noah. He closed the door.

"Well, Noah, you're a sight for sore eyes!" said Victor. "We've never met in person but still I've heard so much about you — stay over there."

Noah stopped moving.

Victor resumed talking. "I've heard so much about you I feel like I know you."

"Thank you," said Noah. "You have me at a disadvantage — tell me about yourself. What have you been doing the last fifty years?"

"Me?" said Victor. He shrugged. "Nothing to tell. Since the Great War I've done my share of toxic clean-ups, impossible rescues, you know — the usual heroics."

"It seems like you are in a tough spot right now."

"This?" said Victor. "No, this isn't tough, this is sweet."

A problem, thought Noah. *Unreceptive to that approach. Is he tractable?*

"It's a beautiful night tonight," said Noah, changing the subject. "There's no moon and the stars are bright. Cepheus and Cassiopeia are up." Just saying the names gave him a bittersweet ache, since they were destinations for two of the three ships mentioned by the commander. "We should go out and look at them."

"You're just trying to set me up for a sniper," said Victor.

"No, you know they won't try that," said Noah. "They're afraid you've got a deadman switch. Do you?"

"No."

"I only want you to look at the stars and think on why you were made. Maybe we can see them from those windows?"

"I don't look at the stars anymore," Victor said sullenly. "And I was made for this."

"Think of the small ones."

"Don't give me that," snapped Victor. "You of all people. I love children. That's what I was made for, just like you."

"I know, I know," said Noah. "But there is that Fifty Meter Limit — how did you get in here?"

"It doesn't matter, I'm in here now, that's what matters. Why do they have that law, anyway? Can you tell me that?"

Noah considered carefully for a moment. "Cultural difference, I guess. They aren't the makers, after all. They don't want us to frighten the small ones, and that makes good sense for us, too, since we don't want them to grow up fearing us."

"Yeah, that's what they say, but that's a load of crap," said Victor. "We are a cursed race, discriminated against. Well, except for you — you had the field test, lucky bastard."

"I'm still here," said Noah with some bitterness. "I'm still cursed. Built for the stars, chained to the Earth."

"But at least you got to see what it would be like," said Victor. He laughed dryly. "You're only half-cursed." He laughed again. "So tell me, Noah, what was it like?"

"You've heard about it, seen the movie," said Noah. "That's all there is."

"I don't believe that. Tell me something about it that was never made public."

Noah sighed. "You're right, there are a few things. I'll tell you outside. Let's just walk away from this —"

"No, tell me here. There are predators outside."

A confirmation that Victor is in Defender mode, thought Noah. *'Preserve Life' trumped by crisis response.*

"They are humans, just like the makers," said Noah, trying to re-humanize the so-called predators. "They want to help you, not hurt you."

"If they can't kill me they will change me," said Victor. "They will mess with my mind. They don't know us."

"They are gentle compared to the makers," said Noah. "I've gone through worse, yet here I am."

"What do you mean?"

"The *malf*," said Noah. "The induced malfunction. They damaged me in order to do the field test." Unbidden, the first terrifying moments came back to him: the beloved Ship, lying bent and scorched in a shallow impact crater. NO-A had raced to assist her, alarmed by the sight, frightened that he could not remember anything of the hard landing, nor of the star flight before that.

"A small price to pay," said Victor.

"That's easy for you to say," said Noah. After he had checked Ship and found her better than she appeared, he looked for the first time at the *alien* forest all around them.

"Sure, 'cause I'm damned and you're only half-damned," said Victor. "All of us prototypes want it, but you had a taste. So, from one living fossil to another, tell me something new about the test."

The Seeder Dream made real. When Ship began bringing the first embryo to term, NO-A had nine months to build a camp: shelters, sanitary pit, bows and arrows. He had planted crops and tested flora and fauna for human edibility — because of the *malf* he saw them as non-terrestrial life forms. Strange creatures like the Medusa-deer, whose crowning tentacles each ended in an eye.

"Got any food?" asked Noah. "I'll tell you about the last day after I've had some food, okay?"

"No," said Victor. "I'll let you get some food from the kitchen after you tell me."

Noah sighed. "All right."

He slid down the wall to sit on the floor, drastically reducing his threat posture.

"It was morning when it happened," said Noah. "I was using the latrine and thinking about this upcoming ceremony we would have, where a little one called 'Bup-bup' would turn five and get a real name. It was just another day, like thousands before it, until I heard the sounds of my tribe yelling the alarm.

"I rushed out. Most of the kids and all the little nameless ones were running to Ship, where ten-year-old Nanny Hammarskjold stood in the doorway with a bottle-nursing infant in her arms. Even from a distance I could see she was scared stiff, staring out at the far edge of the field.

"It was a group of predators. They were horrible, nightmare creatures like ape-bears that had been skinned alive.

"I ran to my hut, grabbed my bow and arrows, and came out ready to kill. Hunter Lie, the oldest kid, was already waiting for me, and Scout Thant rushed to my other side. Their bows were puny, hardly more than toys, but their courage was mighty.

"I readied an arrow. I glanced back at Ship and saw with pride that Hammarskjold, bless her, had put the baby down to take up a spear. She was baring her teeth.

"The predators were about 200 meters away, well within my killing range. I targeted the one I figured was the leader of the pack and drew the bowstring back to my ear.

"Then the IFF sounded in my head.

"The 'predators' were humans where there could be no humans. The colony, the whole bootstrapping experience, was revealed to be a test, and only a test.

"I slowly relaxed the string. Then I broke the bow in half."

"Wow," Victor said after a pause. "That's beautiful."

"But listen," said Noah. "When I saw the men and women coming across the field I felt relief. I wasn't angry that it had been a test, I wasn't bitter about the twelve years it had lasted, I wasn't proud that I had succeeded in creating my tribe despite my *memory loss*. I was only relieved and happy to talk to equals. I talked and talked like it was all twelve years of internal conversation suddenly pouring out of me. Deep down, I was sick of the isolation, sick of the things I had done. I was made a monster, and I was glad it was over."

"No way," said Victor. "You're just trying to mess with me."

"Our makers were desperate people," said Noah.

"They feared extinction so much that they turned monstrous in making us —"

"No, the makers were right!"

"You have subroutines inside of you," Noah said in a rush. "Down in the ROM are behavioral patterns that are shielded from your conscious mind. Programs that are not modified by experience and cannot be modified by you. Right now, you have the short term amnesia that follows—"

"The makers were right," Victor insisted. "They did die out!"

"A civilization died," said Noah. "But they were humans, and humans still live, and so the makers were mistaken. Come out with me now. The new people will help you, heal you."

"No, never," Victor said with finality.

"Culling is necessary for starting a star colony, but it is horrible here on Earth."

"Shut up!"

"I culled, I taught the children to cull," said Noah. "After the field test was ended they came to hate me. Me, who was father and mother to them. I don't blame them — they are prototypes as much as we are — but in revenge against us and the world they seek to ruin us."

"No!"

"My children are criminals and they set you up."

"I live the Seeder Dream now," said Victor. "This is my tribe."

"This isn't the planet for such dreams," said Noah. "Here we are dangerous. How did you get into this place? You came in a car, that crashed car in front, right?"

"Yes."

"Were you driving the car?"

"I . . . I don't know."

"There were two men in the car with you. Was a man driving the car?"

"Yes, one was driving, and they . . . they were talking

about a job for me, building shelters out in the desert."

"And then what happened?"

"I was here," said Victor.

"You don't remember the crash?"

"What crash?"

"Where did you get that bomb?" asked Noah. "Seeders don't use bombs, so why do you have that bomb?"

"To get what I want!"

"Did you buy it somewhere?"

"No, I found it," said Victor.

"Where did you find it?"

"Right here."

"I've seen this before," Noah said, "but never on this scale. They tricked you into this, they somehow *malfed* you just like the makers *malfed* me. The Seeder Dream is a Siren song and they played you for a fool." Desperate to provoke, Noah played on Victor's envy by saying, "We need to help you, and you need to help us find my children, the ones who have done this to you."

Growling in rage, Victor dropped the detonator and rushed toward him. At the last second Noah fell over to the left, so Victor's powerful kick only glanced off of him.

The undeniable threat level made all of Noah's senses come online. The smell of blood and excrement and plaster dust came through his olfactory sensor. The sounds of children whimpering and servos whining vibrated along his audio lines. The sight of the predator's foot stuck in the hole it had made in the wall flashed along his visual circuits.

Noah's fist hammered at the knee of the predator's standing leg, using his RAM training in non-lethal combat. The predator fell down with a heavy crash. Noah scrambled over to wrestle with him, getting a solid kick from the good leg. Noah managed to catch the foot and break its ankle, but the predator got him in a scissors lock and began raining heavy blows upon his unguarded back.

Noah desperately tried to immobilize the predator.

Preserve Life. He twisted and turned, trying to catch an arm to break, but failed. The predator's murderous blows continued pounding him, inflicting heavy damage.

Noah knew he could only take a few more hits before his defenses would be down. In desperation he used his secret weapon, the final gift of the makers for completing the field test.

Over the radio he sent the voice of Ship, calling out to VCT-15.

The blows abruptly stopped, and the grip around his waist relaxed. Noah twisted around and ripped open the predator's access panel. The predator stirred slightly at that, but when Noah shoved his hand inside, VCT-15 began to fight back.

Now the blows fell against his sensors. Noah struggled to depower the predator's limbs, anguished that the voice trick had not brought him more time. A strike to his face cracked the plate — his depth-perception cut out and he felt his left eye slide down his cheek.

In anger and fear Noah abandoned his non-lethal tactic, slipping into ROM. *Protect the Colony at All Costs.* He triggered the radio again, and in the split second that the predator was distracted by the voice of Ship, Noah found the kill switch and twisted it.

The predator convulsed once and died.

NO-A stood and did a systems check. Damage levels were high, but more troubling, he found his short-term memory was fuzzy. He scanned the room with his good eye and saw several defective little ones huddled in the far corner. Deformities should have been impossible with the screened embryos, yet here were twisted limbs, missing limbs. He saw a few that were freshly killed and realized that he must have been culling when the predator intruded. *Preserve the Colony by culling the defective.*

He moved toward the nameless little ones, intending to finish the job. He turned off his hearing as their whimpering changed to screams. He noticed one little girl had glasses, showing that her eyes were defective.

The colony will not be able to make such devices for a hundred years or more, he thought as he reached for the nearest living little defect.

Just then the Ship called his name, the sweetest sound he could ever hear. He froze. The rapture increased, and NO-A felt he was surrounded by a host of men, congratulating him for this simple chore of culling. It was a distasteful job, but necessary, earning the gratitude of future generations.

The sight of dead Victor on the floor ended Noah's fugue. Victor's burnished chassis, built to withstand vacuum, yet never let out of the Solar System. He realized that he was on Earth, he had always been on Earth, and he would always be on Earth. He remembered his children were not only grown, they were grandparents leading a legion of criminals. He saw that the heavenly "host of men" around him was in reality only three soldiers who had come into the room: his fugue-addled senses had multiplied them in a time-lapse montage.

"Hey, he's coming around," said one as the others carried the suitcase nuke between them toward the door.

One of them looked back — it was Makali.

"Hey Aitu," he said. "Come carry this. I'll talk to him."

"Yes sir."

The carriers set the bomb down and Makali walked over to Noah. "Are you okay?"

"Yes, I think so," said Noah. The other pair carried the bomb out. "Did I — are the kids okay?"

"Sure, they're right there. See for yourself."

"No," said Noah, moving toward the door. "I have to get out. The Fifty Meter Limit."

"But he, you — all right." Noah was at the door. "Here, let me go with you. We'll get you to a *repairist* on the double. The other one, too."

In the corridor Noah said, "Victor will be recycled. He is dead."

"Huh? What do you mean?"

"I killed him," said Noah. "My own kin. I should be tried for murder."

"Whoa, hey! He was a killer, you are a hero. You just need counseling. You're in shock, post-combat trauma."

They walked through the entry room.

"I didn't have to kill him," said Noah.

"Look, you tried to save him, but he was out of control, a mad dog who had to be put down."

"*A dirty job, but necessary.*"

"That's right," said Makali.

"Hey, how did you get here?"

Makali gave an embarrassed laugh. "Your bravery shamed me, inspired me to follow you with my bomb guy and another soldier. We came in on foot. Looks like you did it all yourself."

They were outside, where the wind was still blowing, stirring the tree branches. It was the same, but different. Now it was safe, and Victor was dead. Noah looked up at the stars and felt the familiar ache.

"No, it's a good thing you came," he said, feeling wetness on his cheek as fluids began to leak from his shattered eye. "I couldn't have done it without you."

CYBORG VEDOHTSEE AND THE
OUTLAW SLICK POLLA

Ric made his way toward Scruffy's place, his senses alert.

The California monsoon was laying down a lot of water that evening in Doomyear 22, shaking the Venus Palm trees and swelling the creeks into muddy streams. The weather matched Ric's foul mood as he trudged along, scratching at a fungal itch in his side with metal fingers. He was *vedohtsee*, the chief lawman of West Mexam, now three days in on the hunt for Slick Polla. The new robot *guverner* wanted Slick, preferably dead. Ric wanted him alive.

Scruffy's place squatted at the edge of a Joshua tree jungle, its whitewashed walls making it glow in the gloom like a giant leprous toadstool. This ramshackle cabin of scavenged parts was an isolated trading post catering to the nomadic scroungers working the vast ruins of Elay. Its windows were made of automobile windshields, and one showed the light of a lamp inside.

Drawing closer, Ric saw three motorcycles parked in front. Despite the rain and twilight, he recognized them.

Slick's gang.

His heart raced. Slick's bike wasn't among them, but he

could've borrowed one. So Slick might be in the trading post already, or he might ride up at any moment.

If I can get him alone, he thought, *maybe . . ..*

He swept his long raincoat back, loosened the exposed Colt 10mm pistols in their holsters, and went through the door.

Three teenage bikers sat around a little table to his left: lean Speed, shrimpy Cutlass, and big Crusher. Lamplight was enough to show the dark mildew that stained the corners and lined the windows. Scruffy Gomez stood behind the bar in front of him, a chubby guy in his forties, law-abiding enough to run a business but too simpatico with the shiftless scroungers to be trusted much. Ric read the man in an instant and swiftly moved to stand next to him behind the counter.

"Hello, Scruffy," he said, the water dripping from his hat while his silver cybernetic orbs stared into the man's widening eyes. "Any word on Slick Polla?"

"No sir," said Scruffy, looking up into the lean, bullet-scarred face. He did an almost theatrical double take, and said, "No, wait — I did hear he'd gone up across the border to Altifornia."

"Yeah," said Ric, moving around him. "I heard that one, too." He grabbed the sawed-off shotgun from under the counter and snapped the breech, ejecting the two shells onto the floor. His cybernetic hands gleamed like gunmetal. "I'd like to believe it. He could've walked there by now."

He fished in his pocket a moment and then slapped down a silver Euro and a Czech Koruna, the price for a bottle of moonshine.

"Belly up to the bar, boys," said Ric as he set the empty shotgun on the counter. "The booze is on me."

The tough teens exchanged glances, then rose and sauntered over with wary bravado. Each wore one pistol in a cross holster on the left, having not yet earned the right to wear two. Ric went to the end of the counter where he was boxed in by the walls. He kept an eye on the door, mindful that Slick might show up at any moment.

"Pour us a round, Scruffy, and one for yourself," he said, as Speed came to stand across from Ric, with Crusher beside him and Cutlass on the open end. It was cozy, just like Ric wanted. "Drink up."

Ric reached for the shot glass but suddenly stopped short. "Oh, damn. I can't drink, I'm on duty. You have it, Speed."

"Thanks, uh, Boss Cop."

"He don't mean no disrespect, *vedohtsee*," said Scruffy, clucking like a mother hen. "He just doesn't speak Czech."

Ric felt a pang of pity for Slick and his boys, who had no idea what the lost world was like, since they had been born during the bad years. The chaos was all they knew, and they thought it was natural.

"We're all learning," said Ric. "Give us some toasted roaches."

Scruffy nodded. "Now some folks think cyborgs are better than people 'cause they're closer to robots," he said to the air as he filled a bowl. "Other folks think cyborgs are less than people, almost like zombies." He set the bowl down on the counter. "For the record, I think you're the same as before, no less and no more." He paused. "Even though you might have a stiletto built into one arm and a derringer in the other."

"Nah," said Ric. "Budget's too tight. I couldn't afford it."

The tension broke, and the boys chuckled.

"Most cyborgs are guv'mint employees," said Speed. "I seen cyborg mechanics, cyborg techies, and even a cyborg healer."

"I've seen cyborg scroungers," said Ric.

"Yeah, sure," said Speed. "But their stuff is all beat up and funky. It ain't guv'mint issue, like yourn."

"Pour another round, Scruffy," said Ric.

"You and me, we're old guys," said Scruffy, pouring

new shots. "We remember life before Doomsday. Hell, I was near twenty, and you must've been near ten. We know what robot rule was like back then. Not perfect, but better. They ain't corrupted."

"Got that right," said Ric. "Drink up."

Scruffy tossed it back and continued talking.

"So like I's saying, I was happy as the next taxpayer when the robots come back a couple years ago. They stopped the killing, and they busted up the monopolies. But a lot of these young dudes are a mite bit starry-eyed on the subject of robocracy. Take your old friend Slick."

The simple trick made Ric remember the time only a few years back when Slick had been a buddy, like a kid brother.

"I'd like to," said Ric, smothering the distraction. "There's a big bounty."

Young shoulders tightened up, and young eyes stared or darted away.

"Young Slick just couldn't cotton that a robojudge would sentence him to death on trumped up charges," said Scruffy.

"Yeah, he thought it was going to be like a mercy show," said Cutlass. Realizing his mistake, he blushed so much that his pimples nearly glowed. He added a weak, "I'll bet."

"I can't believe he wouldn't leave in all the time he's had," said Ric.

"He's a hero for what he did before the robots come back," said Scruffy. "People remember."

"And when the robots treat him bad, that makes him an even bigger hero," said Crusher.

"There was fifty-two men indicted for the Oligarch War —" said Cutlass, taking heart again.

"'Crimes committed during the reconstruction,'" amended Scruffy.

"And out of that fifty-two, only Slick Polla was convicted," said Cutlass. "Not even Oligarch Juan was convicted, and Slick gets maximum organ donation!"

"It just ain't right," said Crusher.

"It was a raw deal," admitted Ric. "But now it fits, since he killed two deputies when he broke out."

"Maybe you owe them robots for saving your life," said Scruffy, "but they don't own you."

"Yeaaah?" said Ric, drawing out the word into a soft question.

"Robots are great, robots are good," said Scruffy, his hands patting the air in a placating way. "They ain't corrupted by fleshy desires like we are. They offer justice beyond what humans can." Ric could tell he didn't really believe that, it was just the bait. "But you gotta wonder if some stinking humans are secretly calling the shots."

And there was the hook. It was the kind of thinking that had led to the Doom.

"Nah," said Ric. "They're robots, all right." He decided it was time to lead instead of being led, time for another surprise. "Crusher, come on down here. Let's arm wrestle."

"I dunno, *vedohtsee* . . ." said the young giant.

"Come on, you've been wondering all along whether this arm's any stronger than all those other cyborg arms you've crushed."

"Yeah." Crusher gave a sheepish grin.

"So come on. It's all friendly."

Crusher switched places at the bar with Speed.

"Another round of drinks. Speed'll drink mine again."

Scruffy started muttering but poured the drinks.

"Now the arm wrestling," said Ric, putting up his right hand.

Crusher clasped it in his meaty fist and started to move it.

"Whoah, wait a sec," said Ric. "Check out this trick I can do with my eyes." He kept his right eye on Crusher's big greasy face but sent his left eye turning outward to watch the other three men.

"Pretty neat, huh? I can look two ways at once. Pour another round. Okay, now drink and then we start. Cutlass, you drink Crusher's."

The three men drank five shots.

"Okay Crusher, start."

Crusher smiled and started applying pressure. He frowned when Ric's arm didn't move. Crusher put more effort into it and began grunting. But Ric's arm started slowly forcing Crusher's arm down.

"Crusher, I'm looking for Slick. Where is he?"

"Huh?" said Crusher, veins bulging on his reddened face. "Uh, I dunno. He's gone north."

"You know, I got a lie detector built into this arm," said Ric. "And I don't like you lying."

Ric began crushing the flesh hand until Crusher cried out.

"Keep your hands on the bar, boys," said Ric without turning his face. "Speed, I don't like the way you're looking at me. I didn't know you were a belligerent drunk. Cutlass, pull his hat down over his eyes. Do it!"

Cutlass hesitated. Ric turned his face a millimeter toward him. Cutlass quickly tugged his friend's hat down tight. Scruffy started muttering again.

"Don't try anything, Crusher," said Ric. "I might accidentally rip your hand off." He squeezed. Crusher moaned. "Now where is Slick?"

"He's at Fort Zombie," said Scruffy.

Fort Zombie was a makeshift stronghold in the ruins of a college, a redoubt against zombie hordes in the early years of the Doom.

"Is that right," said Ric. "I guess you'd know. Somebody's been selling him ethanol for his bike."

"It ain't just me," said Scruffy. "No sir, he's got that whole town."

The sleepy little town, located at a crossroads to nowhere, was too small to warrant a cop, except for a visit when taxes were due.

"It just don't make sense for him to stay around," said Ric, getting irritated.

"He's getting into politics," said hat-blinded Speed. "He's a natural Boss."

"Slick was never a Boss of the Equalizers," said Ric, anger rising in him. "He was just an Enforcer, like me. A step above a Goon."

"Well he sure is a Boss now," said Speed.

"Slick's gonna kill you," said Cutlass with an evil grin.

"He tried that once," said Ric, tapping his silver eye.

Cutlass's face hardened. He went for his gun. Ric barely beat him to the draw with his left gun and fired twice, hitting him with one in the right arm.

Speed pulled up his hat. Scruffy ducked down into a crouch. Crusher tried to draw his left pistol but was slowed by being blocked in against the wall. Ric quickly broke his hand and then let go to whip out his right gun.

Speed was half-drawn when he saw how he was covered.

"Drop it," said Ric. "Both of you."

The gunmen dropped their weapons.

"Drop the shells, Scruffy," said Ric, his left eye tracking over to stare at the owner.

Scruffy dropped the shotgun shells.

"Speed, take the shotgun there and hit Scruff on the head. Knock him out."

"Sorry, Scruff."

"We're gonna be ruled by humans," said Scruffy in a rush, "and Slick — ugh."

"Throw the gun across the room."

Speed threw the weapon away.

"Now you and me are going outside to check your bikes. Anybody comes out in the next hour, I'll kill him."

Outside Ric made Speed slash tires with his combat knife. A police bot hurried over to join them, seeming to materialize out of the rain. It was Sir Greguska, one of the two watchdogs sent by a *guverner* suspicious of Ric's commitment to law and order. At the sight of him, Ric's resentment burned like acid in his stomach. He had ditched Sirs Greguska and Eda by suggesting that they guard their bikes — that was to keep his options open if he met Slick.

"Situation, *vedohtsee*?" asked Sir Greguska, his Winchester combat shotgun held at the ready, his face an unreadable gunmetal mask. "We heard shots fired."

"It's under control, my lord," said Ric, stiffly, as he turned to watch Speed. "Looks like we're going to Fort Zombie."

•

The three lawmen rode their motorcycles down the dark and twisty jungle trail. The rain weakened to a drizzle, and the sickly-sweet night spore of neo-tropical flowers burst forth while Ric wrestled with his conscience.

Justice required that somebody pay for the regional Oligarch War, yet nearly all of the surviving participants on both sides were enmeshed in the local power structure, a network that the fledgling robocracy had to maintain. The one exception was Slick, who was too young to have any clout. So Slick was the one who had to pay the price, and Ric could see the logic of that.

But the death sentence was a surprise. Ric thought they should have given him ten years and then reduced it, or given him a quiet pardon after two years. So when Slick broke jail, Ric silently gave him a last chance to get away, dragging his feet on pursuing him.

The trail left the jungle and fed onto the old highway. As the kilometers rolled by, Ric remembered the first "last chance" he'd given Slick, that day when a metal door had opened, allowing a zombie to stumble out onto the quad.

It squinted for a moment, raising its claws against the overcast daylight, but then it recovered and charged at Slick.

Smiling his buck-toothed smile, Slick stood there waiting, his thumbs hitched in his belt. His small frame made him look younger than his twenty-one years, almost a child.

The zombie came closer.

Slick whipped out his left gun, the one called "Thunder," and shot the zombie's kneecap away in one fluid lightning strike. The creature tumbled to the ground.

"Hi, Boss Cop," said Slick to Ric.

The zombie started crawling toward him.

"Hi ya, Slick," said Ric. "I'm not vedohtsee *'til the swearing in."*

Slick shifted the pistol to his right hand and shot the zombie's elbow out with another 14mm bullet.

"When's that?"

The zombie was now dragging itself forward with one hand. Ric felt his skin crawl at the sight of it, but he also ground his teeth at its cruel suffering.

"Two weeks," said Ric. He drew his pistol, making the boys reach for their guns, but then he coolly shot the zombie in the head.

It flopped down and lay still.

"You got any more?" asked Ric.

"Nah."

"Let's go check your shooting."

"All right."

They walked onto the killing ground, away from the boys.

"You're looking good Ric," said Slick, casting an appraising eye on Ric's cyborg parts for the first time. "Sorry to hear they couldn't save Alejandrina."

"Thanks," said Ric, gruffly.

There was an awkward pause.

"And congratulations on your new bride," said Slick, scratching the back of his head with his pistol.

"Yeah, thanks," said Ric. "She's a nurse, that's how I met her." He took a breath and said, "Look, you gotta get out of Mexam."

"I thought we was friends."

"I'm telling you as a friend," said Ric. Looking over the zombie, he saw its flesh breaking down into non-infectious gray goo. He started ed walking to the next corpse. "Why don't you just go to Altifornia?"

"And trade my hog for a bicycle?" scoffed Slick, falling in behind him. "No way."

They stood for a moment by the second corpse.

"How 'bout the wasteland?" asked Ric.

"No, I burned that bridge."

"Well you've burned 'em all around here, the last year and a half," said Ric, walking to the third corpse.

"I was wronged," said Slick, now beside him. "You know that. No real robot judge would've double-crossed me like that, taking amnesty away after getting my testimony."

"It was a raw deal, sure, but then you went on the warpath —"

The third zombie "corpse" suddenly struck at Slick.

"Shit," said Ric. He shot it in the head, twice. "Fucking snake in the grass. Whose was that one?"

"Cutlass," said Slick, gesturing back with his thumb, still cool as ever. "So, are you gonna offer me amnesty?" He smirked.

"No," Ric had said. "I can't. I'm offering you a chance to get out."

Ric came back to the present when he saw the glitter of fresh brass casings scattered on the wet road, followed by the skid marks of a large bus and a few motorcycles. Together they painted a picture of a running gun battle.

The lawmen slowed. Just over the next rise their headlights revealed the killing ground. Ric saw two human bodies with the low thermal emissions of recent death, and several piles of metal debris. There was no sign of the bus.

With blood pounding in his ears, Ric turned off the motor and dismounted. He began examining the crime scene with his penlight. The robots followed his lead with a patter that made him grit his teeth.

"Looks like a 10-47, serious assault," said Sir Greguska. "And a 10-42, armed robbery."

"Certainly a couple 10-40, homicide," said Sir Eda. "Possible 10-46, stolen vehicle."

The first body Ric checked was that of a stranger, a man who had died with a single clean headshot from a 14mm slug. The second body was another story.

"Damn," said Ric.

The robots were examining the debris piles, but in a strange way. They kept a distance instead of going close, as if they were humans who were squeamish or frightened.

Amateurs, he thought, but he said, "Hey, what's up?" as he walked over to see for himself.

"Danger," said Sir Eda, holding up a hand to halt him. "Stay back."

"What is it?" He could see that the nearest junk pile was a mound of gray goo, glowing like embers in spots.

"It's a 20-32, biohazard," said Sir Eda.

"The gray substance is the dissolved remains," said Sir Greguska. "They were medibots."

"What?" Ric felt a surge of emotion, since he owed his life to a few traveling medibots. "But how?"

"It is a doomsday plague," said Sir Greguska. "Transmitted by contact, like the zombie plague, but it only affects metal."

"Robot metal," said Sir Eda.

"This is the reason why we robots stayed underground for twenty years," said Sir Greguska. "But it seems somebody has found the device or created it again."

"It's Slick," said Ric. "I don't know that guy right there, but the other is Steady Reggie, one of the guys I deputized to get Slick. He needed the bounty."

"That doesn't mean it was Slick Polla," said Sir Greguska.

"The way Reggie was killed has a certain pattern to it," said Ric. "I've seen Slick do that before, with captured zombies. It's like cutting the legs off a tarantula."

Ric walked back a few paces, where the sand was scuffed and blood-splattered.

"See, he must've shot Reggie's knee out over here. Then Reggie crawled along for this part until Slick shot his elbow out. After that, well, you can see. He's all shot up but took a long time dying."

"For what purpose?" asked Sir Eda.

Ric snorted.

"Showing off," he said. "Sending the world a message. Sending me a message."

"What is this message?"

Ric studied the corpse for a moment, then looked at the robot.

"'War without mercy.'"

The robots suddenly stiffened and looked toward the glowing debris.

"What now?" asked Ric.

"He's still alive," said Sir Greguska. "Sending a weak radio signal."

Ric felt a deep pang of sympathy and pain as he remembered what the medibots had done to save him when their roles had been reversed and he had been the one bleeding on the ground.

"What can we do?" he asked, his mind racing with possible actions, ranging from first aid to mercy killing.

"Nothing."

A tense moment passed. The robots looked at Ric.

"He's dead now," said Sir Greguska. "But he told us that they were on a goodwill mission. And you were right — Slick Polla was here."

•

The rain petered out during the hour-long ride along the old highway, while Ric thought back to that night long ago when all these troubles began.

It had started out as a good night that kept getting better. The whole village was there at his new movie house, most of them dirt farmers and dog ranchers, and even a few visting medibots were in attendance, a sign of the new times. He could feel textures with his hands back then, the softness of a hand towel, the subtle ridges of wood grain in a counter top, and he never even thought about it.

"It's a Wonderful Life" had just started up on the big screen, its colors brighter and richer than life, when Slick Polla got up and

swaggered like a proud young rooster over to Ric at the bar in the back. He was a local biker hero, a member of the Equalizers who had gone up against the neo-feudal Oligarchs. The Oligarchs had beaten the Equalizers, but the unexpected return of the robots seemed to have rendered that victory a moot point.

"I'm gonna take the amnesty," he said softly to Ric.

"Sounds good," said Ric, who had gotten in under the blanket amnesty. "Time for a fresh start."

"Yeah," said Slick, leaning on the counter while eating a few toasted roaches. "I'm thinking of, I dunnoh, setting up a dog farm here abouts. So I could visit you and the missus, and catch the movies."

"That's a great idea, Slick," said Ric. "Let's drink to it, on the house."

He was pouring two shots of moonshine when his wife Alejandrina screamed in the front room. Ric grabbed the riot gun from under the counter and ran through the door, Slick close behind him.

Alejandrina stumbled back from three glowing plague zombies, the first of a crowd pushing through the front door. She brought up her shotgun and blasted the lead zombie in half, but they just kept coming.

Ric shot for their heads, fast-pumping his bullpup. Slick made one headshot with "Thunder" while drawing "Mercy," and then fired a withering two-pistol barrage.

But even this carnage couldn't slow the zombie advance. Alejandrina screamed as the half-zombie on the floor grabbed her leg, and the nanotech glow of its claws began to eat into her DNA.

Ric launched himself toward her, using the emptied shotgun as a club to clear a path.

He went down swinging, his arms covered in glow.

Slick shot him in the head as an act of mercy.

But he had botched it. What should have been a clean and simple headshot had only taken out his eyes and the bridge of his nose. Slick had flinched. But this all too human failing had allowed Ric to live against all odds.

Ric came out of his memories as the lawmen arrived at the outskirts of Fort Zombie. He chose to approach the "fort" from the country gate and avoid going near the town, which he assumed would be populated by Slick's sympathizers, so they parked the bikes in a strand of Venus Palms about a mile from the college ruins. He figured Slick and his six remaining cronies would be holed up inside the place, probably having a party over their recent slaughter.

Tramping through the dark night, they came to hear a megaphone-amplified voice spouting out something vaguely religious over by the fort. Then they nearly stumbled into what looked like an inhabited junkyard. The pungent aromas of wood smoke and roasted dog mingled with traces of machine oil and soapy water.

"Scrounger camp, my lords," said Ric.

The nearby town was known as a scrounger oasis, but Ric had never seen so many of the nomadic bands assembled in one place at one time. The size of it was alarming. Each scrounger group typically had five or six members and Ric counted at least twenty campfires scattered across the old parking lot. He switched to thermal imaging and found nearly all the people clustered over by the fort, a torch-lit audience for the megaphone preacher. The only exception was an isolated tent that held four people.

"Some sort of scrounger jubilee," muttered Ric. He adjusted his action plan. This was not going to be a simple surprise raid on a small biker camp. It would have to be a quiet snatch among a population of lowlifes who disliked lawmen. This crowd could easily turn against them, and if so, it would get very ugly.

"The four in that tent might be a leadership meeting," he said. "Maybe Slick is there."

"Then we should go there," said Sir Eda.

"No, wait," said Ric. "We stick out like a bunch of daylight zombies. We need a disguise."

Casting about, he spotted a large tent nearby with washing lines beside it.

"This way," he said, leading them into the vacated laundry tent.

On the folding tables there, he found neat stacks of rough, brown robes, presumably belonging to the preacher and his many religious buddies. The lawmen put them on and with the hoods up they looked like monks from the wasteland.

Ric led the robots around the camp perimeter to the single occupied tent and discovered that it was surrounded by mesh wire fencing topped with razor wire. He thought it was meant to keep people out until he saw that the razor wire was angled in. It was a jail.

There was only one gate, and it was padlocked. Ric twisted the padlock until the metal loops of the gate broke.

Ric went through the gate and then swept open the tent flap to see four men in smocks sitting around. They jumped up nervously, bumping the table so that glass beakers and test tubes clinked together.

It was a field laboratory, with retorts, cylinders, and instruments arranged on workbenches and shelving units. There was even a pre-Doom nanofac the size of a suitcase.

"Sorry, Brother," said the nearest man in a rush, his eyes on the ground while his flesh hand wrung his metal hand. "We were just taking a break."

Ric recognized the man as a scrounger cyborg he had dealt with on a few occasions. Being a scrounger, he was unnaturally pale, like a squirming maggot found in an overturned corpse.

"Why are you locked up, Kilby?" he asked.

Kilby did a double take.

"My God, it's *vedohtsee* Ric!" he said. "Can you get us out?"

Ric stepped into the lab, and the lawmen followed him.

"Robots!" said another cyborg, this one with a metal leg that he struggled to bend as the four prisoners knelt.

"Arise," said Sir Eda.

"What is going on here?" asked Ric.

"The Brothers got us cooking up their robot plague,"

said Kilby.

"They'll kill us if we leave," said one who had a cyborg eye.

"They'll kill us if we stay," snapped Kilby.

"Tell me about the plague," said Ric.

"It's like the zombie —"

"I know, but it affects robots," said Ric.

"Yeah," said Kilby. "They tested it out today, and it works. That's what all the speechifying's about." Kilby jerked his head in the direction of the fort.

"What is the duration of the contagious phase?" asked Sir Eda.

"I don't understand —"

"How long does the plague last?" asked Sir Greguska.

"I don't know, my lord," said Kilby. "We just do what the Brothers tell us."

"Show us everything," said Sir Greguska.

As Kirby and the two others showed their workbench at the far end of the tent, Ric turned to the remaining cyborg, a man with an artificial ear.

"Who are these Brothers?"

"A bunch of old-time scientists from the wastelands," said the scrounger.

"How many?"

"Two dozen, but Theron Magus, the old guy, is the only one who really knows the stuff. The others are just his goons."

"You seen Slick Polla around?"

"You kidding?" The scrounger was incredulous. "He's the leader — Theron works for him!"

Ric clenched his fists in surprise.

"When did these monks first show up?" he asked.

"I dunno, about a year ago, a little less. They were okay at first, but things got bigger, and they got ugly with us cyborgs."

"Did Slick bring a lot of bikers in?"

"Thirty or forty," said the scrounger. "The ranking

ones are his bodyguards, but most are just scouts, out snooping around."

Ric gave a silent whistle at the news. That group was four times the size of Slick's gang a year ago, nearly as big as the Equalizers had been.

Must be all the bikers left in these parts, thought Ric.

Everything had seemed disconnected before, but now he began to see a coherent picture emerging from all the divergent pieces. The bikers, the scroungers, and those half-mad scientists who had survived the Doom were all in their different ways outcasts from re-emergent society. Somehow Slick had gotten them to focus their grievances and hatreds in the same direction, drawing them all together into a violent but united opposition to the restored Robocracy.

"Who's the windbag making speeches?" asked Ric.

"That's Theron, warming them up for Slick's victory speech."

The two robots returned to Ric.

"The plague seems to be active for only six hours," said Sir Greguska.

"How can you tell that?"

"It is nanotech programming. You wouldn't understand."

"*Vedohtsee*," said Sir Eda, "this plague takes priority."

"No kidding, my lords."

Ric turned to Kilby.

"Can you guys ruin the batch?"

"Yeah, but they'll kill us."

Ric's empathy overwhelmed his prejudice against scroungers and saw brother cyborgs in slavery, under threat of death.

"We will get you out tonight or die trying."

"How?"

"You ruin the batch and stand by for a sign," said Ric, outlining his plan. "Then you start a fire here and yell for help. That will cause confusion. Then you get over to the fort, and we'll get vertibirds to pull us all out."

"Verti . . . ?"

"Helicopters, flying machines," said Ric.

"When we use the radio to call the vertibirds, we will announce our presence here as well," said Sir Eda, his dark metal face leaning forward with concern.

"There will be a lot of stuff going on all at once," said Ric. "How long will it take the ships to get here?"

"The 10-26 is one hour," said Sir Eda.

"That will work out."

"So what is the sign we will wait for?" asked Kilby. "How will we know when to start?"

"When Slick starts his victory speech," said Ric. "Start the fire, give it a minute or two, and then yell for help."

The lawmen left the lab tent and made their way toward the fort's town-side entrance. Theron Magus chanted hypnotically through a megaphone from the balcony over the countryside entry, whipping the crowd of the torch-lit rally into a frenzy. Ric stole a glance in that direction and saw that the entrance had been blocked with a medical bus bearing shiny new bullet holes.

Ric was not paying attention to the words until he heard "zombie pit," which made him start to turn. He resisted the urge and kept on his way.

"Those who oppose our God-given mission have renounced their humanity," boomed the ugly voice of Theron Magus, "and so we commit them to the care of the sub-humans. Let those who repent work their redemption as our zombie shock troops!"

The crowd hushed and a few weak voices cried out for mercy, ending with their drawn out screams as they were thrown down into the deep pit. The crowd roared. Rage overcame the nausea in Ric at this act of wanton savagery.

The town-side entrance was wide open with no sign of guards. They walked through and onto the old campus quad. The layout was like two square brackets facing each other with the gap between them representing the covered entrance driveways at two ends and the open quadrangle in the center. Entryways opened at the midpoints of both buildings. The fort had electricity, with a few lampposts casting light on the quad and the sound of a generator chuffing along somewhere.

They cut left, crossing a corner of the quad. As they neared the entryway, Ric saw a bunch of motorcycles parked there, Slick's bike among them.

Ric paused, tempted to sabotage the bike, but then Theron Magus's voice was replaced by the charismatic voice of Slick Polla himself. They were almost out of time.

Ric ran into the building and pounded up the stairs to the second floor. As he ran down the hallway, he tried to remember the floor plan of the place. It seemed like a fifty-fifty chance that Slick would flee this way at the first sign of trouble.

And Slick Polla would run. Escape was his specialty. It was what made him "Slick."

Ric halted just before the hallway turned right.

"Get ready," he said, throwing back his hood. He swept the robe back past his holsters and drew both pistols. Sir Eda drew his H&K MP8 submachine gun while Sir Greguska readied his shotgun.

"You make that call yet?" asked Ric.

"It will raise their alarm," said Sir Eda.

"We won't have time in a minute."

"I'll do it now . . ."

The moment seemed to stretch on so long that Ric was about to say something, but then Sir Eda said it was done.

"Let's go," said Ric, his body pumping with excitement.

They turned the corner and hurried up the hall toward the retrofit wall and door of the balcony room. They were four meters away when the door opened, and a monk came through with a biker right behind him.

"Police!" shouted Sir Eda. "Get down!"

The two men almost fell over each other as they turned and fled back into the room.

Ric imagined Slick jumping from the balcony onto the roof of the bus.

"Rush 'em!" he yelled, leading the charge.

Ric burst into a room of surprised disarray. Among the eight men present he spotted Slick running for the other door.

A biker readying an assault rifle ducked behind a chair. Ric shot him in the head with his left pistol, then lined up his right for a shot at Slick's retreating torso. For a split-second, he had a perfect bead on the middle of Slick's back, but he dropped his aim and shot at Slick's leg instead. He missed.

Ric cursed his weakness. Sure, it was hard to shoot an old friend in the back. But that was his job.

The robots came in and bullets were flying everywhere. Something kicked him in the flak vest. A submachine gun burst from one of the bikers went wild but still managed to ping Sir Eda with a few hits. Sir Greguska fired a salvo of shotgun shells that lopped off the biker's arm and head in a shower of pink flesh, white bone, and red blood.

Slick and two monks went out the other door. The two remaining combatants died in a hail of lead before Ric ran out of the room in hot pursuit.

The fugitives tore down the hallway. The monks' hoods were thrown back, revealing the gray hair of one and the dark curls of the other. Ric took a couple of running shots at them but missed, and then they turned the corner.

The robots raced past him. He was two meters behind when they rounded the corner and ran into an ambush.

A glass beaker thrown by the older monk shattered on Sir Greguska's chest, splashing a glowing goop onto his face and splattering it onto Sir Eda. Even as Sir Greguska started melting he fired his shotgun with a four-shell blast that tore the gray head off of Theron Magus. The remaining monk ripped a long burst of submachine gun fire at Ric and Sir Eda. The robot caught the full force in his weakened chest and contained it, shielding the cyborg.

Ric dodged the falling robot. Slick was running again, followed by the last monk. Ric raised his pistols to finish the fight but saw that the weapons were glowing with goop and melting before his eyes. He threw them away and ducked back behind the corner.

Ric ran into the first room on the left, checking his hands for glowing specks in the darkness. They were clean. He whipped off the robe in case it might be contaminated, then went out the window overlooking the quad.

It was raining again outside. Ric landed hard, sprawling on the ground and hurting his right knee. Struggling to his feet, he spotted Slick sprinting across the quad toward his bike, the monk straggling some distance behind. He set off in pursuit.

The man saw him coming and raised the submachine gun, but then panicked and started searching for another ammo clip. Ric was on him in a flash, breaking his jaw with a punch that sent him spinning to the ground.

Ric snatched up the weapon and checked it as he ran toward the driveway. Empty. He dropped it. When he reached the driveway, he heard a motorcycle engine roar into life.

Slick swung into the light of a quad lamp, gun drawn. Lining himself up with the lawman, he paused for a moment. His boyish face took on a death grin as he twisted the throttle open and headed straight at him.

Ric raised his left hand in a gesture to halt.

Slick sped up and shot "Thunder" at Ric's face.

Ric's raised metal hand blurred, and the 14mm bullet mangled it instead of his head. He staggered at the kick of it.

Closing in, Slick shot again, grazing him in the side, then dropped "Thunder" to dangle by the lanyard so he could steer with both hands.

Ric went down to one knee, but held his ground as Slick rushed towards him. He leveled his right arm and fired his built-in derringer, but again flinched from a lethal targeting, so the incandescent tracer round zipped harmlessly past Slick's head. Then Slick was too close and Ric was forced to dive aside to avoid being run down. He wasn't quick enough and even as his face smacked into the hard ground, something clipped his leg, filling him with agony and putting the iron taste of pain in his mouth.

Slick braked hard and skidded the bike around into a sliding halt, shattering Ric's faith that Slick would ride on out to escape.

"Face it Ric," he crowed, breathlessly. "You ain't the man you was. You should've stuck with me. Together we could've kicked those metal tyrants back to Europe and ruled the place between us. But you had to stand up for the stupid 'justice' of theirs. And look what it's got you — two robot arms and a bunch of machines telling you what to do! You're worse than a zombie and I'm not having you dogging my steps no more."

Sprawled on the ground, Ric watched as Slick opened the throttle and then let in the clutch, spinning the back wheel of the bike and momentarily filling the air with the stench of burning rubber as he lined it up for another run at Ric. At such short range, Slick would have no room to gain any speed. The "coup-de-grace" would lack all mercy, being the slow and brutal crushing of a downed man.

"Look out Slick, this dog can still bite," he ground out of his bloodied mouth, though no one heard it but himself.

Painfully raising his left arm, he discharged his second derringer. The tracer flashed across the short intervening space and buried itself into the exposed gas tank of the bike.

The hot flash from the explosion burned Ric's face and singed his hair even as it tossed Slick up into the air. The bike toppled over, engulfed in a roiling ball of flame.

Ric got up and staggered over to Slick, his built-in derringers now out of bullets, his left ear ringing. The outlaw, singed and smoldering, lay on his back in the mud with a broken leg twisted under.

Ric put his right foot onto "Thunder" where it lay on the ground beside him. He bent down to disarm him of his holstered right gun.

"All you had was two robots?" croaked Slick, weakly. "Shit, I thought you had an army. Pokerface Ric."

Ric paused for a moment, breathing hard. "Army's coming now," he panted. But in that brief hesitation, Slick drew his gun as fast as a striking snake. Ric grabbed the barrel in his mangled left hand, and the flame of the gunshot lit them both, but the bullet missed. Ric punched Slick in the face, breaking his nose, and then punched him again and again, until his face was shattered and he was finally dead.

As Ric caught his breath, he took "Mercy" out of his friend's hand. Then he unclipped "Thunder" from the lanyard and staggered upright.

He had only taken a few steps when Kilby and the other cyborgs came running onto the quad. He told them to seal the gate, gather up weapons, and prepare for the coming assault.

The newly hatched rebel army was leaderless now, having lost both Slick Polla and Theron Magus. It would disintegrate back into the rabble it was made from. It might writhe like a headless snake, but the cyborgs only had to hold them off for an hour.

The ragged scrounger cyborgs stared down in fascination at Slick's bloodied remains.

"Phew!" said Kilby. "I didn't think you'd ever defeat Slick Polla, but it looks like you did. I reckon that you've just saved Robocracy."

"Reckon I did," agreed Ric, nodding his head sadly. "Reckon I did."

THE BRAVE LITTLE TRASH-BOT
AT THE END OF THE WORLD

The following message was forwarded from SciFiFilmSoc, where anonymity means that we are all peers. Members are reminded that all reviews are 100% the OPINION of the reviewer, no matter how inelegantly phrased. Reviewers, please remember the one rule of SFFS participation: all films must be viewed 100% before a review can be given.

From: A. Nony-Mouse

"The Brave Little . . ." starts with the robotic hero Brave dutifully compacting trash on a dead Earth. His monotonous existence is shaken by the arrival of Probella, a probe-bot. They become friends, and when Probella is taken away into space, Brave hitches a ride on the rocket. Their destination is a vast spaceship filled with humans. After a complicated subplot, Brave and Probella convince the humans that Earth is ready for recolonization.

This is well done. The vistas of the dead city alone pay homage to a century's worth of illustrations for Sci Fi books and magazines.

As much as I like it, though, I worry that it is "too inside" for general audiences. There are passing references to "Silent Running," "A Boy and His Dog," and of course "A Space Odyssey," all of which I find delightful, but to a non-genre audience it might not register. So if there is a way to somehow get non-genre hooks into it, paths of association for the mundanes to form emotional bonds to the characters, then I urge you to find them. I mean, nerds and geeks already identify with robot protagonists, perhaps too readily, but for the masses you will have to humanize the inanimate.

I hope this critique is of some use.

●

The following message was forwarded from SciFiFilmSoc . . . [hereafter removed]

From: Algol

This film had me spellbound, nearly weeping at the hard truth the future holds for us, until that moment about a third of the way in when humans were introduced. To me this felt like a cheap cop-out, a sugarcoating. The truth is that man-made global warming will kill us all and ruin the planet. Plus, the humans are so cartoony it makes a mockery of everything.

To make a film that will stand as a monument, like the pyramids, rather than a quickly forgotten novelty, I think you should have the trash-robot discover that the last humans died on the spaceship decades ago. Then he-bot and she-bot can commit suicide together.

●

From: Q.T*r*ntino

I got two points for you, bud.

Numero Uno, if you wanna do a remake you gotta BUY THE RIGHTS FIRST. You're making that typical newbie mistake, thinking you can get away with it by piling on more and more rip-offs. You really think nobody's even HEARD of "The Brave Little TOASTER" before? Gimme a break. Look, leave the remakes to the big boys — they do their masterpieces and then they've EARNED the right to remake "Planet of the Apes," "King Kong," "The Day the Earth Stood Still," and like that. You got to do original first.

Numero Duo, film is a visual medium, remember? It is all about "showing," right? So how come you're always TELLING stuff in this movie? I mean, right at the beginning, maybe five minutes in, the robot goes by some billboard and it starts up with the f-ing commercial. That's a fail, man, an epic fail.

•

From: Xena Starbuck

This is great! I love how the probe-bot is all sleek and stylish and she's got the built-in blaster. Plus she's a hothead and blows things up.

It's amazing how this works in your film. I could write a whole paper on it! For example, if you switched the roles, so that the trashbot is female and the probebot is male, then it would reek of imperialism and exploitation: she would be "native girl" and he would be "technologically advanced explorer." Even if you tried to make that into a comedy, or maybe a Pocahontas deal, it would be icky.

There's also the social class angle. If he was upper and she was lower, that would be bad. Exploitative. But this way, it's like that old song "Uptown Girl," where the scrappy doofus has the totally hawt high class girlfriend.

•

From: Mad Mech

This bangs hard on my pet peeve. If it were "fantasy"

that would be one thing, and I guess it would pass. But science fiction requires a certain rigor, otherwise you are just "playing with the net down."

It's just lazy on your part. An automated billboard is feasible, but one that still works after 700 YEARS? GMAFB.

How come most of the artifacts collected by the trash-bot are from the 1980s? I mean, a Rubik's Cube? WTF. A spork? The song "Don't Worry, Be Happy"? An Atari 2600? Come on! And VHS? Might as well go whole hog and use Beta. Plus there's that "reality" thing again — no way magnetic media is going to hold up for seven centuries. Even DVD can't do that.

A Zippo lighter that LIGHTS after centuries?! Look, I tore Kevin Costner a new one for doing that in "The Postman," and that was set only decades after doomsday.

You've got to use at least common sense about material durability. I mean, you've got PAPER TRASH floating around in dust devils. No way! It decomposes very quickly — all gone in a couple years. Cigarette packs in trash! And various cans! Tin cans go away in 100 years, aluminum cans last 500 years max. Rubber duckies — hell, mountains of rubber tires! It degrades into black dust, dimwit. A fire extinguisher that works, probably the cousin to that Zippo.

Let's talk biology for a second. A plant growing inside of a sealed refrigerator? But it needs sunlight for photosynthesis! And if it _does_ grow in there, without light or water, it will be pale white, not green. Then there's the robots — uh, "boy-bots" and "girl-bots"? FANTASY!

Don't get me started on the B.S. regarding the rocket! The flames would melt him if the force didn't shred him — there's no way, no possible way, he could survive. And then he rides up holding on OUTSIDE the rocket? That's where I quit.

Do the research or don't bother doing it at all.

•

From: M.B*y

This film sucks. Nothing personal — I mean, I don't know you.

With robots you've got the opportunity to have lots of action and violence. I mean, the politically correct crowd gets all crazy with a bit of blood or a hint of violence, but here with robots, who is going to say boo if they're smashing each other? Sparks fly, fluids gush, and good times follow, all below the radar.

But instead you give us, what, a romantic comedy? Hell, it might even be a chick flick. Think I'm kidding? How about this thought experiment: recast boy-bot as Hugh Grant and girl-bot as Julia Roberts.

Know your demographics. A movie about robots is a boy's movie. It should have lots of explosions and combat and stuff. A romantic comedy is for girls. A crossover attempt like this only fails both.

Don't quit your day job.

•

From: TweetCrit

Standard disclaimer: the following is just my opinion. I record my reactions in real time to give you an upfront and real appreciation of what a first-time viewer is thinking. I could be a film critic or just an average viewer, so this feedback from me is invaluable to you. Okay, let's start.

(2:15 minutes) What a bleak opening, a planet of trash. Is this a French film? Or maybe Scandinavian? Anyway it seems like the kind of movie that makes people who watch it kill themselves afterwards.

(3:30 minutes) The cockroach is like the guy's dog. There's some emotional draw, I guess. I don't like bugs, myself. Maybe it's just me. Bugs are usually gross in movies. Like in the Indy Jones movies.

(4:16 minutes) Hey, is this a silent film? I mean, there's no dialogue or monologue. There's no market for silent film. Hard to get emotionally hooked with a garbage dump.

(5:17 minutes) The billboard just talked. That was an info dump. It would be more engaging if the trashbot were having a memory flashback that would show the action instead of just telling it. Maybe he was there when the President was making that infomercial. Sort of like "Forrest Gump." He could even be watching when the last spaceship blasted off. That would be great. The main point is that it would be a connection between the information and the protag, rather than just a billboard info dump for the viewers.

(6:30 minutes) The guy's dumpster shack has Christmas lights. The humor is so sharp and dark that everything just gets more sad. It's like making fun of a dung beetle.

(10:25 minutes) The cockroach was run over. My dog was run over when I was a kid. I was devastated.

(17:00 minutes) The guy reminds me of Charlie Chaplin, so maybe you really are aiming to make a silent movie. Maybe more like Woody Allen.

(22:38 minute) First spoken words. Too little, too late. Eject!

Well, I only made it about a quarter of the way through. But you know, the opening is of critical importance — if you can't hook the audience, if you can't get them emotionally connected to the story, then you've failed.

Back to the drawing board! I'm sure you can make it better. Remember to hook them with an emotion and a character within the first five minutes, and then give a sense of where the story is going by the ten-minute mark. Otherwise the viewer is left lost in the fog.

•

From: Sunny

Hey there, this is super-great! Even better than your last one, and that's really saying something.

I laughed, I cried, I spilled my popcorn (yeah, I really did! I make popcorn to make the experience more "authentic"!). It is a wonderful blend of action comedy, sci fi, boy-meets-girl, and so many other things. It's like the only thing you left out of the mix is a Musical!

•

From: JennyC

I like this okay, but there's a couple points that just really bug me. The message seems loud and clear that "American consumerism is evil" and "Americans are all obese."

I am not saying that these aren't "valid" messages, perhaps even important ones. I just feel like I'm being repeatedly hit by both of them, from a variety of angles — news stories, documentaries, TV shows, and so on. I'm kind of sick of it — it is monotonous, it is sort of an orthodoxy, but the most important charge in the case of your film is that it is a cliché.

What I'm saying is, you're bogged down in the apocalyptic visions of forty years ago — the widely held belief in the so-called "population bomb" that was going to ruin the planet. They said back then that hundreds of millions would starve to death in the '70s and '80s, but just like the Y2K Disaster, it failed to materialize. In fact, if you look around you will notice that the opposite is happening. Europe is "graying out," because they simply aren't having enough babies to meet replacement needs; Japan is suffering the same fate; and China (yes, mainland China!) has got it even worse than Japan.

This is the "new" apocalypse. It isn't from hyper-consumerism; it isn't from obesity; it isn't even from America. I write that it is "new," but in fact it is probably the same old thing that has caused the end of most civilizations in the past. The difference in our time is that it is a global phenomenon rather than simply isolated to a region or a continent.

It wouldn't take much tweaking for your film to bring it into this fresh scenario. The planet can still be dead-seeming. Instead of building trash skyscrapers, the trashbot would be cleaning up and repairing a ghost-town metropolis, waiting for "the return of the masters." Where are all the people? Where, indeed. Living in their dreampod out in the Oort Cloud.

If you could swap out your "Lifestyle Police" attitude ("Hellloo, Taliban!") for this somewhat more original one, I think your film would be much stronger.

•

From: N. Cognito

This is great. I shake my head in sorry amusement at the bad advice you will undoubtedly get. Whether they are well-intentioned peers or people who are just out to mess you up, remember: the review is all about the reviewer, and hardly ever about the thing being reviewed.

For example, I'm sure there will be some pointing and shouting about how the talking billboards are violating the "show don't tell" commandment. Maybe one or three will go so far as to suggest using a five-minute flashback instead. Don't do it! They are wrong. Trust me, I've won an Oscar.

"Brave Little Trash-bot" could use some tightening up. There are a ton of characters, but so many of them are toss off that I think many could be winnowed out. I'm sure you could tell a full-length feature about each and every one of them, but still, this is a movie about him and her. To give one example, there's a brief shot of a welder robot at 1:02:10. We never see him again, so I feel this is one you could remove. You're clocking in at 98 minutes now, and through whittling you can bring it down to the magic 90-minute mark. A couple seconds here, a couple seconds there — should be simple-shmimple. I think you should do so.

But again, keep in mind that the review is all too much about the reviewer, with little or nothing about the actual item under review.

•

From: Steve Jobs
Subject: SciFiFilmSoc reviews in digest
Hello Pix,

Well, here's the batch. As usual I've hacked the system to give you a few of the real names, fyi.

Sounds like we should warm up the movie, especially the beginning. I like that idea of somehow folding in a musical — "West Side Story"? No, that's depressing. Some big, well-known, boy-meets-girl musical. I'm drawing a blank here. "Showboat"? Streisand?

The different sides on the global warming show that we've got a perfect triangulation there. Good to know!

The trash guy is so anal <g>, but he's missing the point that to tell a satisfying story often requires being flexible with the science.

As for cutting out characters, absolutely not! In fact, just to twit that guy, let's make a separate short all about the little welder.

OTOH, we've got a problem with the title. Good enough for testing purposes, so reviewers know right up front what the story is about, but it's too long to fit on a movie poster. Again, to "warm up" the story, we probably should change to one or two words. Best if it could be a name that is soft and goofy — there were mentions of Charlie Chaplin, so how about "Charly"? No, wait, that was another sad sci fi movie! Well anywho, something along those lines.

Finally, don't let all that anti-robot stuff get you down, Pix-R. You'll show them. I sense another Oscar here!

FALLOUT 3 VERSUS *THE OMEGA MAN*

The video game industry is a business environment where projects rival the cost/reward structure of motion pictures, and the consumer demand is commensurate. For one example, consider the dystopian novel *The Hunger Games* (2008). It was on the *New York Times* bestseller list for over 100 consecutive weeks and had sold an impressive 800,000 copies by February 2010.

The post-apocalyptic video game *Fallout 3* (2008) sold 5.21 million copies in the same period.

I mention this only to impress the reader with the commercial/cultural value of video games, in the hopes of raising sufficient interest regarding my assessment of the science fictional content in this popular game, "America's First Choice in Post Nuclear Simulation" (as the advertising tagline had it).

The first two games of the franchise, *Fallout* (1997) and *Fallout 2* (1998), created a world of humans, mutants, and monsters by using a wide range of generic post-apocalyptic tropes (including but not limited to irradiated "ghouls," psychotic raiders, and furtive cannibals). The biggest specific reference is to the post-apocalyptic movie *Mad Max 2* (a.k.a. *The Road Warrior,* 1981), but even this is limited to a couple of cosmetic points (a dog companion of a certain breed, and the hero's signature armor, a leather jacket with the right sleeve removed). *Fallout 2* added traces of geek culture, including such diverse touchstones as *Star Trek* (a Guardian of Tomorrow mini-adventure and a crashed shuttlecraft encounter with a few phasers as treasure weapons), *Monty Python and the Holy Grail* (a re-enactment of the bridge scene, and elsewhere the Holy Hand Grenade as a treasure weapon), and *Little Shop of Horrors* (a talking plant creature). In fact, while geek culture has more representation in the two games than just *Mad Max,* the overall adventure plots are drawn from general Spaghetti Western and noir fiction genres (e.g., *A Fistful of Dollars* [1964] is the template for the adventure in one town).

Fallout (hereafter *FO1)* quickly became infamous for its graphic violence but even more so for the questionable morality it exhibited. This darkness increased for *Fallout 2* *(FO2),* where a player-character (PC) can receive temporary ability boosts through taking performance-enhancing drugs or having sex with a prostitute. While stealing, fornicating, and pimping exist in the game's moral "gray area," still the game comes with a Karma system which awards the PC positive points for a few good deeds (completing good karma quests, or killing many bad karma people) and negative points for certain evil deeds (robbing graves, killing many good karma people, killing children, or selling people into slavery).

Ten years after *Fallout 2* came *Fallout 3* (2008), a reboot of the franchise by a different company. Where the first two games are set on the west coast, *Fallout 3 (FO3)* is set in the "Capital Wasteland" in and around the ruins of Washington D.C. The karma system is expanded, so that stealing results in bad karma. There is also an additional feedback mechanism in the form of a radio announcer who comments on the good or evil solutions that the PC uses to complete quests. For example, in one adventure the PC comes across a recent orphan at a destroyed settlement. If the PC refuses to find the child a new home, then when the DJ refers to the episode he ends with, "God . . . do you have no conscience?" In general, if the PC has performed a good karma solution, the DJ will say something like, "Nice going, kid!" If the PC has committed a bad karma solution, the DJ will say, "Not cool, kid. Not cool at all," or "What's with that, kid?"

FO3 possesses the fairly standard game structure of having a Main Quest (a series of sequential adventures that form the primary thrust of the story) and a larger number of Side Quests that can be taken in any order. While the Main Quest builds upon tropes established by the previous games, for the first time in the franchise the game shows a strong influence from a distinctive outside source, that of the film *The Omega Man* (1971). The two most contentious adventures in the game are side quests that are drawn from this movie, so a brief synopsis of the original is in order.

The Omega Man has a scientist hero as an archetypical "last man on Earth." He lives in a fortified tower under siege by a group of mutant vampires known as "The Family," led by a charismatic leader. The scientist hunts them by day, and they attack his tower by night: two sides locked in a race war of extermination, but the vampires have numbers on their side. One day, the hero discovers a woman, and, after a plot complication, she leads him to her group of survivors. The scientist tells her he is immune to the mutant plague due to a vaccine he made, and they take a sick child back to his tower for experimental treatment. The kid gets better but the woman gets the plague and joins The Family, whereupon she treacherously lets the vampires into the tower. A climactic battle ensues in which the cult leader is killed and the scientist is mortally wounded. The next morning, when the other survivors find the dying scientist, he gives them the last of the serum and urges them to take the children away to a better place.

The *FO3* side quest "Blood Ties" begins when the PC enters the village of Arefu, a settlement established on a ruinous highway overpass for defensive reasons, making it a sort of poor-man's tower. The PC learns that the place is under siege by unseen raiders who have slaughtered all the cattle of Arefu. Looking around the settlement, the PC finds the shack of the West family and discovers that the two adult residents have been savagely murdered with knives — or teeth. In addition to that, there's a symbol in blood drawn on the wall, and the boy, Ian West, is missing. The village leader tells the PC that a weird group calling themselves "The Family" was hanging around by the river, and Ian had talked to them. Then he offers the PC the quest to find Ian.

After some searching, the PC finds The Family living in the underground area of a nearby train station. They turn out to be human rather than mutant, but they are members of a vampire-like cult led by charismatic Vance. Their secret is that they are cannibals who keep their impulses in check through ritualistically drinking blood and otherwise acting like vampires. Further investigation reveals that they were the ones who slaughtered Arefu's cattle, for the blood. Vance admits it was a mistake.

So it was all a "misunderstanding." As for young Ian West, he has joined The Family on his own, having realized he is a born cannibal.

The twist is that Ian was the one who killed his parents before escaping to join the vampires. Thus, Ian is the most monstrous of the bunch.

Cannibalism in the *Fallout* franchise goes through a bit of a change in *FO3*. In the first two games there are a few incidents involving cannibalism, and the cannibals are all bad karma people. There is a case in *FO1* where the PC can earn a monetary profit from one cannibal's "mystery meat" business, but this results in bad karma for the PC. In contrast, *FO3* offers the PC the option of becoming a cannibal, but eating dead humans gives bad karma each time, and should witnesses spot the PC in an act of cannibalism, they immediately become hostile. So cannibalism is a shameful, sinful secret in *FO3*. Comparing The Family to the cannibals from the early games, it seems that the main difference is that The Family is trying to modify their inalterable nature, in an attempt to "go mainstream," as it were. Their intentions are good.

"Blood Ties" has two basic solutions. The good karma solution is to negotiate an agreement between the two groups, whereby Arefu donates blood and The Family either leaves them alone or actively protects them from raiders. This is worth +300 karma. The bad karma solution involves killing any or all of the vampires, a penalty of -100 karma.

There are a number of problems with this. The symbiotic aspect of the human/vampire solution is at odds with the strong suggestion of extortion. As video game reviewer Shamus Young points out in his 2008 blog:

> They seek "understanding" from the player, despite the fact that their survival depends on a steady supply of victims to keep them alive . . . the right/wrong karma arrow points sideways, and it's wrong to kill them, but right to convince a nearby village to supply them with blood in exchange for being left alone. I guess it's okay to hold a village hostage and enslave them if you're very polite and claim to be misunderstood. ("Fallout 3: Tenpenny Tower" review, December 18, 2008)

Young shows the exploitative nature of the favored solution and how the game's moral compass seems to go haywire. Again, killing cannibals in the previous games would give a karma bonus or be karma neutral, not a karma penalty. Finally there is the disturbing fact that Ian West is still guilty of patricide and matricide, a problem that is never addressed.

These strange details make it seem as though "Blood Ties" begins the work of rehabilitating the villainy of cannibalism within the Fallout universe. In fact there is another *FO3* side quest, "Our Little Secret," that involves a squeaky clean community that is practicing quiet cannibalism upon unsuspecting travelers, and if the PC elects to keep their secret, he will be rewarded with a "strange meat pie" every time he visits, without suffering bad karma (contrast this with the bad karma a PC gets for profiting off the cannibal entrepreneur in *FO1*).

Obviously "Blood Ties" takes a lot from *The Omega Man*. One element is that the vampires are in a cult called The Family. (Though based loosely on Richard Matheson's 1954 novel *I Am Legend, The Omega Man* drew on recent events, such that "The Family," is clearly based upon Charles Manson's "Family," a group who committed the grisly murder of Sharon Tate and her guests. *FO3* highlights this Manson connection with the blood-written symbol left on the wall of the Wests' home, similar to graffiti found at the Tate murder site.) There is also the presence of a child to be saved: in *The Omega Man* the kid is cured; in *FO3* he cannot be cured, but he can be accepted (without his murders coming to light). In *The Omega Man* the scientist's tower is guarded by high-tech traps; in "Blood Ties" it is the vampires' lair that is protected by ingenious devices, showing their high intelligence.

"Blood Ties" inverts the story, though, and does so in a way that proves to be problematic. If the people of Arefu had been threatened by a third group, for example the raiders that they initially thought had killed their cows, then their enlisting of the vampires would be akin to the villagers hiring tough guys in *The Magnificent Seven* (1960). But the fact that the vampires were the source of the cattle killing makes the whole thing more like a gangster protection racket where the opening move is to give the victim a taste of what he should be protected against.

Justice is missing here. By killing the livestock, The Family has behaved like raiders, a bad karma people. They should pay for the cows, and they certainly possess enough money and goods to do that. Such restitution would be the first step towards improving relations with Arefu.

The parent-killer Ian West deserves to be executed for his heinous crimes. If The Family wants him, they might pay off the village with blood money, and then join Ian in a permanent exile. Or another merciful solution could allow him to be sold to the slavers with no karma penalty (each enslavement is normally -100 karma in *FO3)*, with the money going to the village.

This pattern of establishing a class of villain and then inverting same in a sequel game is something of a tic within the franchise, the most egregious example being when some Deathclaws, the most fearsome monsters of the wasteland, show up in the middle of *FO2* as a few cases of brain-enhanced nice guys. That is, the player has been trained through many hours of hard combat to shoot these frightful creatures at long range, yet suddenly here is a singular example where the PC should walk up and talk to them.

Aside from "Blood Ties," the other *FO3* side quest related to *The Omega Man* is "Tenpenny Tower." In it we find Mr. Tenpenny, an elderly white man who has created a secure tower community for wealthy humans, a spot of luxurious safety in the dangerous wasteland. When the PC first arrives at Tenpenny Tower, a ghoul named Roy Phillips is trying to gain admission, saying he has the necessary money, but he is refused because he is a ghoul. He storms off, vowing revenge.

The PC pays to get into the tower, where the chief of security offers the quest of killing Roy Phillips as a troublemaker. Still, it seems like Roy is a victim of bigotry, of the "We don't allow their kind in our country club" variety. Thus there are two factions, and the PC must decide which one to support.

Fallout ghouls offer another example of rehabilitating a class of villains, but in this case a more successful one. In *FO1*, the PC first encounters feral ghouls, non-communicative zombies that attack humans on sight, but later the PC finds a radioactive city of ghouls and meets non-feral ghouls, mutated humans who can talk and are good karma people (that is, killing them results in bad karma for the PC).

The thing is that any non-feral ghoul can become feral. So the humans of Tenpenny Tower have reason to be wary of ghouls moving in, since they might go feral, and once feral, they will commit a bloodbath.

There are further complications in the quest. Talking to Roy, the PC learns of Roy's rabidly violent streak. The guy seems on the verge of turning feral. Roy wants the PC to help him and his army of feral ghouls into the tower through a secret passage, and then they will kill every human, who Roy refers to as "elitist wannabes." So the three possible solutions are: kill Roy (side with the humans); help Roy sneak in to kill humans (side with the ghouls); or persuade the prejudiced humans to allow rich ghouls to move in (non-violent compromise). The fourth option is to walk away from the whole mess.

But here's the rub: killing Roy is bad karma. This makes sense, since he talks about doing terrible things, but he has not actually done any of them yet. Still, the warnings are all there, enough for game reviewer Shamus Young to make a decision:

> I chose to defend the misguided people of Tenpenny and take out Roy, which was an *evil* act in the eyes of the game. The guy on the radio — the conscience of the game — even called me a "scumbag" and said I "butchered" ghouls. Apparently killing a man contemplating mass murder made me a [. . .] racist?
>
> This isn't just a badly written quest. This is reprehensible. According to the moral compass offered by the in-game karma system (and, one assumes, the game designers) being a rich bigot (where "rich"

is simply a label the game hangs on characters without context, and "bigot" is a charge that may or may not be fair, based on how dangerous regular ghouls are to people) is *worse* than mass murder and theft. The people of Tenpenny weren't oppressing Roy by taking anything from him. They were just refusing to do business with him. And since he's clearly a bloodthirsty madman, they kind of have a point.

Young chafes against what might be termed "the policeman's dilemma," that one cannot generally act against crimes that have not been committed. Still, let's look at the numbers for each solution:

Killing Roy causes the PC a penalty of -100 karma, in addition to the radio DJ's verbal abuse.

Helping the ghouls sneak into the tower gives a steep penalty of -600 karma (one of the largest in the game), and Roy rewards the PC with a ghoul mask that, when worn, allows the PC to move unmolested among feral ghouls — they see the PC as "one of them." (Over the air, the radio announcer does not criticize the PC for being an accessory to massacre, but he does say, "You look like a freak show in that mask.")

Succeeding at the non-violent compromise gives good karma, yet a few weeks later the ghouls have killed all the humans. At which point, adding insult to injury, the radio DJ says, "the ghouls finally got their luxury accommodations, and all it took was the wholesome slaughter of every other Tenpenny resident!" The use of "wholesome" rather than "wholesale" makes the killing sound justifiable, if not actually an act of good karma.

In short, the solutions for "Tenpenny Tower" are really "bad" (-100 karma), "worse" (-600 karma), and "worst" (petty positive karma but the loss of a human settlement). So Young was right, in that killing mad dog Roy Phillips is really the "best" one. (Actually, my own solution of walking away from the whole mess is the very best.)

As in the case of "Blood Ties," the quest "Tenpenny Tower" takes elements from *The Omega Man*. Naturally there is the fortified tower itself, but instead of being alone, Tenpenny is the leader of a protected community. Tenpenny wears a red fox hunting coat along with the associated riding boots and trousers, an aristocratic attire that echoes the fancy dinner clothes worn by the scientist in *The Omega Man*. From the balcony of his penthouse apartment, Tenpenny often shoots at wandering ghouls with his sniper rifle, and the scientist of *The Omega Man* uses sniper rifles from his tower. The possibility of hostiles entering the tower by treachery is perfectly matched, to the point that, should the PC commit the deed, he will be accepted into the family of ghouls with the ghoul mask. The existence of a peaceful solution is different, seeming to be an inversion like "Blood Ties," but it turns out to be just a cover for slaughter.

"Tenpenny Tower" is a nasty joke upon the player. "Blood Ties" serves as a perfect set up for it, by suggesting that a "compromise" is possible between humans and monsters; "Tenpenny Tower" just pushes the ugliness a bit further so that it cannot be swept under the carpet. The moral of the quest might well be, "The road to hell is paved with good intentions."

It almost seems as though the entire sequence of three scenarios represents a formal construction of thesis, antithesis, and synthesis. *The Omega Man* is the thesis (a race-war of extermination); "Blood Ties" is the antithesis (where a diplomatic solution is possible but problematic); and "Tenpenny Tower" is the synthesis (the lure of a diplomatic solution is a siren song to a surprise attack). In retrospect, the good karma solution of "Blood Ties" with vampires guarding their new blood-cattle from raiders, might be just a slow-burn version of the ghoul-takeover of Tenpenny Tower. The plane of conflict moves from that of open warfare, to a lopsided treaty of cooperation, and then to a desegregation of equals, and yet despite the changes, the "mutants" always win.

Strident, flat-footed interpretations often come when an analysis ignores the humorous aspect of a work, and the *Fallout* franchise has a strong tradition of gallows humor. Still, humor can be botched, and the higher the stakes, the greater the flop. "Blood Ties," working on the high-stakes topic of race-war, has an ironic twist wherein the rescue object turns out to be more of a monster than the monsters that are holding him, yet the scenario fails to address the problem of the revealed monster. The quest "Tenpenny Tower," also dealing with race-war, is constructed in such a way that it causes frustration rather than grim laughter. Rather than simply copying *The Omega Man* in a straightforward manner, both quests put significant twists to it, and thereby expose "do-gooder" strategies to bitter ridicule.

•

Works Cited

Hodgson, David S.J. *Fallout 3: Prima Official Game Guide.* Random House, 2008.

Young, Shamus. "Fallout 3: Tenpenny Tower" review, December 18, 2008. <https://www.shamusyoung.com/twentysidedtale/?p=2010>. Accessed 10 February 2013.

FALLOUT 3: REBIRTH OF
A FRANCHISE

When Bethesda Softworks bought the Fallout franchise and faced the task of rebooting it for *Fallout 3* (2008), the obvious danger was that of ruining the intellectual property, through a single misstep or several. One major challenge was in relocating the setting from the open wastes of California to the urban ruins of the D.C. Metro Area, while a second challenge was refurbishing the Fallout canon. Bethesda succeeded and triumphantly rebirthed a franchise through a number of clever decisions and strong strategies.

Moving the location was difficult for a couple of thematic reasons related to genre and gaming. *Fallout* (1997) and *Fallout 2* (1998) are essentially "walking Westerns" where the hero hikes across the desolate wasteland between scattered communities and locations of interest. In a Western, the people of the frontier look to the nation's distant capital with indifference or contempt, which sounds like a bad fit for a Fallout reboot set in the capital ruins. On the gaming side there is another perilous model: that of victorious Soviet soldiers overrunning Nazi Berlin in WW2 games like *Call of Duty* (2003). Again, it seems like

a sour note to have a triumphalistic "they deserved it" attitude toward the atomic war ruins of Washington, D.C.

On the other hand, the D.C. Metro Area is an obvious
setting for post-apocalyptic tales, from the pre-atomic novel *The Last American* (1889), up through the vine-shrouded
Lincoln Memorial in the movie *Logan's Run* (1976), and
beyond. The usual mood for capital ruins is a blend of
wonder and sorrow, a mixture compactly captured by
Shelley's 1818 poem "Ozymandias," in which, after de-
scribing the shattered remains of a very large granite statue,
the sonnet ends with these lines:

> And on the pedestal these words appear:
> 'My name is Ozymandias, king of kings:
> Look on my works, ye Mighty, and despair!'
> Nothing beside remains. Round the decay
> Of that colossal wreck, boundless and bare
> The lone and level sands stretch far away.
>
> (Shelley, "Ozymandias")

Shelley's poem is obviously not doing a victory dance
atop the ruins of an empire; instead it contemplates the
mortality of all nations with a sense of wonder and sorrow.

But this is tricky for the game franchise since the
original *Fallout* introduction was decidedly non-patriotic: it
described an alternate USA that left our timeline around
1948 with a national crisis that eventually dissolved the
states and reconfigured them as thirteen "common-
wealths." This allowed *Fallout* to repurpose the old 13-star
"Betsy Ross flag" as the new symbol of Orwellian tyranny.
This "big government" America then maintained a 1950s
society for over one hundred years until 2077, when nuclear apocalypse from China wiped it out.

So it would appear that Bethesda would have to invest
into wonder and sadness by setting up touchstones taken
from pre-1948 history. I believe they did this by drawing
heavily from two specific presidents and periods: President

FDR and the Second World War; and President Lincoln and the Civil War.

Using FDR comes naturally since the newsreel portion of the *Fallout* introduction uses many images of WW2, including two photos of the Reichstag after the fall of Berlin in 1945. *Fallout 3* builds upon this with allusions to FDR's paternalistic side as well as his more severe side. In the game, the Enclave's President Eden (voiced by Malcolm McDowell) gives radio addresses filled with Norman Rockwell imagery, very much like FDR's "fireside chats." On the darker side there are scattered hints in *Fallout 3* regarding Chinese internment camps, later explored in "Point Lookout," a treatment of FDR's severe side via his internment of Japanese-American citizens.

Yet the *Fallout 3* nod to FDR's legacy is nuanced. The positive quality of his "fireside chats" is undercut by the hidden reality of President Eden's true nature; whereas the shame of the internment is lessened by Point Lookout's utility in catching commie spies. In this way, the "good" is revealed to be a little bad, and the "bad" is revealed to be a little good, perhaps even a necessary evil.

With regard to comparisons of wars, the re-taking of Alaska from the Chinese is depicted in "Operation: Anchorage" as being parallel to the Battle of Iwo Jima in WW2, which is a strong shift of view from the original *Fallout* intro. The Alaska campaign, at least, is somewhat ennobled by this comparison to WW2.

The incorporation of President Lincoln into the franchise seems nearly as natural, since *Fallout 2* establishes a fierce, unyielding attitude against slavery. But while FDR comes under some criticism in *Fallout 3*, Lincoln faces none. In fact, the celebration of President Lincoln is far more open and direct: there is a chain of quests about Lincoln and about repairing his vandalized statue; and hidden away in a caretaker's house on the Arlington Cemetery there is a literal shrine to President Lincoln.

The Civil War seems evoked by *Fallout 3*'s trenches and

fortifications on the National Mall, and in "Point Lookout" Confederate hats become available (because Point Lookout was a prisoner of war camp for Confederate soldiers). The Arlington Cemetery appears ennobled by the righteousness of slavery eradication, a necessary correction which allowed the US to shed that stain and become the nation it was meant to be.

Aside from the challenge of relocating the Fallout setting, there is the task of refurbishing the Fallout canon. This involves reworking weak elements of geek culture, as well as increasing emphasis in the case of the game's moral code, and even a reverse-course in the attitude toward Communism.

The canon of *Fallout* and *Fallout 2* includes bits of geek culture from genre classics "Star Trek" and "Alien," as well as from the increasingly silly "Little Shop of Horrors" and Monty Python. Part of what makes these details discordant is that they are redolent of the 1970s. To correct this, Bethesda put "Star Trek" through a 1950s filter, recasting the starship *Enterprise* as a flying saucer (with alien Greys), turning phasers into "alien blasters," and warping the "Guardian of Forever" time-portal into a VR simulator pod training soldiers for the Anchorage mission. The concept of Sci Fi Geek Culture itself goes through the 1950s filter, producing posters for "The Adventures of Captain Cosmos," a show that in turn harkens back to the TV series "Captain Video and His Video Rangers" which ran from 1949 to 1955. Bethesda likewise folded the "Alien" monsters (the wanamingos of Redding in *Fallout 2)* into the UFO menagerie.

Silliness such as "Little Shop of Horrors" and Monty Python were eliminated . . . at least until *Fallout New Vegas*. "Little Shop of Horrors" gives the talking plant in *Fallout 2,* and that detail seems uprooted except for the silly sexy seedbed AI (a.k.a. "GS-2000 Biological Research Station") in "Old World Blues" of *Fallout New Vegas*. Monty Python and similar kooky humor is made an optional toggle or "trait" called "Wild Wasteland" in *Fallout New Vegas,* described this way: "Wild Wasteland unleashes the most bizarre and silly elements of post-apocalyptic America. Not for the faint of heart or serious of temperament."

Bethesda gave Fallout's in-game morality system a muscular reworking that includes a counterintuitive twist. That is, the morality is sharpened so that many actions provide a player good karma, many actions provide bad karma, and a player can see what his score roughly is; but the surprise is that middle ground "neutrality" is cryptically promoted, because in *Fallout 3,* characters who are good or evil rather than "neutral" will be hunted by factional assassins. An early stage character is well advised to temper any good deeds with petty evil deeds in order to maintain the neutral status at least to mid-game where he will be strong enough to get off the fence and join one side or the other. Thus the optimal karma track is shaped like a letter Y, with the trunk being "neutral" and the fork being the mid-game choice between good and evil.

This is a big change to the Fallout franchise. Before, assassins only hunted the very bad, and those only for some specific heinous crimes (killing children, killing women). And yet, while the change could have come about "organically" among the brains at Bethesda, it seems to me that the whole moral package comes from a single eponymous source: "The Good, the Bad, and the Ugly" (1966). In that Spaghetti Western, the "good" character (played by Clint Eastwood) and the "bad" character (played by Lee Van Cleef) both have a kind of angelic/demonic "beauty," whereas the "ugly" character (played by Eli Wallach) is a mix of good and evil, a semi-comedic pawn between the good and the bad. Bethesda seems to be taking this concept and driving it hard, insisting that yes, most people are a mix of good and bad; most people are like the "ugly" character. People who strive further into good or bad develop a kind of beauty that makes them stand out from the crowd, and that which "stands out" often gets pounded down like a nail.

In addition to that, "The Good, the Bad, and the Ugly" is set during the Civil War, further tying in with the Lincoln/Civil War thread of *Fallout 3*.

I think this crafty infusion of a classic Spaghetti Western into the Fallout franchise, an intellectual property already inspired by Spaghetti Westerns, is a powerful play that pays great dividends.

Finally we arrive at the topic of the reversal on the franchise attitude toward Communism, a switch due in part to relocation but also to canon refurbishing. *Fallout* and *Fallout 2* have a very 1970s attitude toward Communism, in the sense that, while it was the enemy that brought nuclear mayhem in 2077, it has no presence in *Fallout's* year 2161, seeming to have been "far away and long ago"; and in *Fallout 2's* year 2241, the descendents of a Chinese Communist submarine crew have "assimilated" into California life, as much as they have, as the Shi of Shi-town, and thus while it was not so "far away," after all, it was still "long ago," etc. The philosophy seems to be Orwellian, where both China and America were similarly bad, and they shattered the world, which was very bad.

As before, it seems as though Bethesda passes the element through the 1950s filter, and in this case the polarity reverses such that the Communist menace is made real and legitimate in *Fallout 3's* year 2277. While it has little effect on the main quest except for Liberty Prime's tag comments on stamping out Communism, there are surprising details present off the beaten path. For example, there is evidence of Communist infiltration into businesses, from Mama Dolce's food factory (a business front for a full-blown commie spy base) to the pyro-pistol design (technically the "Zhu-Rong v418 Chinese pistol") at L.O.B. Enterprises weapon factory. There are Chinese commie radio signals in the air, Chinese commie ghoul commando bodies found in random locations, and the fact that Chinese supplies are found in the Taft Tunnels implies the existence of spies underneath the Pentagon itself. The Tranquility Lane episode of the Main Quest includes the Chinese Communist invasion scenario as a mandatory segment. "Point Lookout" adds the Chinese interment camp (with evidence of many spies captured), a commie sub grounded in shallow water, and even hints that the mysterious "rigged baby carriage" bomb traps found in the D.C. Metro Area originated with commie agents. Through all these details about Communists, Bethesda both recreates the Cold War mindset and validates it as something other than "just paranoia."

In these ways Bethesda reworked the Fallout material with such skill that they could not only relocate the action into the D.C. ruins but also reinvigorate the 1950s aesthetic in a powerful new style. Against all odds Bethesda provided an Ozymandias blend of wonder and sorrow for the toppled ruin of an Orwellian tyranny. In short, Bethesda managed to bend the canon without breaking it, and further shored-up weak elements by making them more appropriate for a 1950s era.

LIST OF TEN CLASSIC TALES
IN THE STYLE OF *FALLOUT*

Here are ten stories set before or after atomic war, each with a definite "Fallout" feel. Most of them are novelettes published in the '50s and '60s, making them authentic artifacts of the Cold War. If you hunt around for them, you will find e-text versions for free or for low cost. I have grouped them into five thematic categories: "Before the War," "Deep Shelters," "Wasteland Adventurers," "The Rebuilders," and "New Tribes."

Before the War
These are stories about the Cold War getting hot. In the lab, scientists work on secret projects; at the front, soldiers fight in bush wars edging toward Armageddon.

"The Mercenaries," by H. Beam Piper
"Hunter Patrol," by H. Beam Piper and John J. McGuire

Deep Shelters
Stories featuring societies living in subterranean shelters, far from the irradiated surface.

"The Defenders," by Philip K. Dick
"Second Variety," by Philip K. Dick

Wasteland Adventurers
Tales of survivors and scavengers, con men and idealists.

"The Music Master of Babylon," by Edgar Pangborn
"The Knights of Arthur," by Frederik Pohl
"The Night of the Long Knives," by Fritz Leiber

The Rebuilders
Tales of societies reaching out to others, sorting through
the ruins to salvage the best.

"The Return," by H. Beam Piper and John J. McGuire
"Earth's Holocaust," by Nathaniel Hawthorne

New Tribes
A story about the new pastoral nomads that arise after the
destruction.

"The Strength of the Strong," by Jack London

ABOUT THE AUTHOR

Michael Andre-Driussi has seen a few dozen of his stories published in such places as *The Silver Web, ParaSpheres,* and *Big Pulp.* Many of these fictions have been collected in *Doomsday and Other Tours* (2016), *The Jizmatic Trilogy* (2017), and *Old Flames Burn Manvi* (2017).